KISS AND TELL

When Ginny agreed to take her sister's place as au pair to two children on a skiing holiday in Austria, she wondered what she'd let herself in for. She'd been warned that Gareth Chilton, the children's uncle and guardian, was an arrogant — if good-looking — man, and was soon to experience his supremely overbearing manner! But Gareth's tender loving care for his niece and nephew melted Ginny's heart like snow in summer. And that was when her problems really began . . .

Books by Diney Delancey
in the Linford Romance Library:

FOR LOVE OF OLIVER
AN OLD-FASHIONED LOVE
LOVE'S DAWNING
SILVERSTRAND
BRAVE HEART
THE SLOPES OF LOVE
THE SECRET OF SHEARWATER

DINEY DELANCEY

KISS
AND
TELL

Complete and Unabridged

LINFORD
Leicester

First published in Great Britain in 1985

First Linford Edition
published 2007

British Library CIP Data

DeLancey, Diney
    Kiss and tell.—Large print ed.—
Linford romance library
    1. Love stories
    2. Large type books
    I. Title
    823.9'2 [F]

    ISBN 978–1–84617–904–4

Published by
F. A. Thorpe (Publishing)
Anstey, Leicestershire

Set by Words & Graphics Ltd.
Anstey, Leicestershire
Printed and bound in Great Britain by
T. J. International Ltd., Padstow, Cornwall

This book is printed on acid-free paper

1

An insistent knocking brought Ginny Howard to the front door of her flat. She knew who it must be demanding entry; only her sister Katie knocked like that. She opened the door and a radiant Katie waltzed in, clutching her sister by the hands and swinging her joyously round.

'Katie! What's happened?' cried Ginny. 'Let go, idiot, you're making me giddy!' She broke free from Katie's grasp and closed the front door before following her sister's joyful progress into the living-room. Katie was so excited she seemed unable to keep still. She perched for a moment on the window-seat and then jumped to her feet again to crush Ginny in a bear-hug.

'It worked,' she cried. 'It worked! And I'm so happy Ginny I feel as if I could explode.' She laughed with delight and threw herself down on the sofa.

'It's Don,' said Katie. 'We're engaged.'

Ginny let out a cry of delight. 'Katie! That's marvellous. Congratulations. I'm thrilled for you.' Both girls were on their feet again, and Ginny hugged her younger sister.

'This calls for a celebratory drink,' she said. 'I've some wine in the fridge — we'll have that.' She went into the kitchen and drew two glasses of wine from the winebox she kept in the fridge. She was glad she had something to offer Katie, for this, she knew, would be the last alcohol she would keep in the flat for some while. She carried the glasses back into the living-room and paused for a moment to look at her sister, once more perched on the window-seat, gazing out at the walled garden below. A shaft of afternoon sunshine fell upon Katie's face, touching her creamy skin with gold and striking flashes of red in her thick dark hair. She was always attractive, but today, clothed in happiness and sunlight, she was beautiful.

Ginny crossed the room and handed Katie a glass. 'Here's to you and Don,' she said, smiling. 'I hope you'll always be as happy as you are today.'

'Oh, I'll drink to that,' said Katie fervently, and took a long pull at the cool wine.

'Now, tell me all about it,' demanded Ginny, settling herself in her chair once more; and so Katie told her.

'The thing was,' she explained, 'I knew I loved him right from the start, and I thought he loved me, but he'd never say so, never commit himself. So when I'd waited long enough . . .'

'How long was long enough?' asked Ginny with a grin.

'Oh, months and months,' said Katie cheerfully. 'Anyway, I decided I couldn't bear the uncertainty any longer. I didn't want to face him with an ultimatum so I thought I'd try shaking him up a little.'

'What did you do?'

'I got a job for the Christmas holidays.'

'A job?' Ginny was puzzled.

'Yes. I decided that if I went away for a while he might realise how much he missed me.'

'Or find someone else,' pointed out Ginny.

* * *

Katie looked serious for a moment and then said, 'Well, that was a risk I had to take. I just felt I couldn't go on as we were. Anyway — ' she smiled — 'it worked. When I told him I was going away for the whole of the Christmas holidays he was horrified and asked me not to go. I said I was afraid it was all arranged, and I'd have to go. Then he said he'd been going to ask me to marry him at Christmas, and when I just stared at him in amazement, he said he supposed he'd better do it now instead. So he did and I said yes.'

Ginny shared in her sister's happiness and said again, 'I'm really thrilled, Katie. Don's a super chap. I hope you'll be very happy. Have you told Mum and Dad yet?'

Katie shook her head. 'No, we're going down at the weekend. They know we're coming but they don't know why. I came to tell you because I just had to tell someone or burst!'

'I'm glad you did. Are you still doing this job you arranged?'

Katie stared at her sister for a moment and then said, 'Oh dear, do you know, I haven't given it a thought since Don proposed?'

'I can understand that,' said Ginny, 'but you'll have to, you know. What was it anyway?'

'Looking after children.'

'But you spend your whole life doing that,' laughed Ginny. Katie was a teacher in a London primary school and faced a class of forty nine-years-olds five days a week.

'I know,' said Katie, 'but it's what I know how to do. Anyway this was quite different because I was going to Austria with them on a skiing holiday.'

'Skiing! Come on, Katie. Begin at the beginning.'

So Katie explained. Don's mother had a friend whose daughter and son-in-law had been killed in a car crash a few weeks before; a motorway pile-up in the fog. They'd left two children aged about seven and ten. It wasn't she who'd been left as the children's guardian, however, but her son, their uncle.

'This is their first Christmas without their parents, and Mrs. Chilton wanted it to be entirely different from the ones which had gone before. Anyway, she arranged with her son Gareth, the children's guardian, that they should take a chalet in Austria and spend Christmas and New Year there. The old lady is a bit arthritic, so she can't actually look after the children on her own. That's why she decided to take a sort of au pair.'

'And that's you?'

'That's me.'

'But how did you hear all this?'

'That's the funny thing. Don told me.'

'And you went and asked for the job?'

Katie nodded.

'Cheeky thing!'

'Well, I was getting desperate and it seemed to be the solution. Mrs. Chilton was very nice and said I seemed to be just the person, particularly as I love the skiing.'

Ginny smiled ruefully. 'Yes,' she said, 'I certainly envy you that. What happens now? Have you told Don you won't go?'

'Well, I suppose I have really,' conceded Katie. 'They'll have to find someone else. I'm sure it won't be difficult, lots of girls would jump at a free skiing holiday with money to spend at the end of it!'

'You must tell her at once so she's got time to advertise,' said Ginny.

Katie sighed. 'Yes, I suppose I must. I only hope she's there on her own. The son, Gareth, was there when she

7

interviewed me and I didn't take to him at all. You know the sort — good-looking in a flashy sort of way, dark hair and smouldering dark eyes.' Katie giggled and rolled her own eyes suggestively. 'A bit arrogant — obviously considered himself very superior. Probably thinks he's God's gift to women.'

Ginny laughed. 'I know the sort,' she said. 'Typical male chauvinist!'

'Exactly.' Katie grinned.

'Well, you'll have to hope they don't mind too much,' said Ginny, 'but I should tell them as soon as possible so they can try to get someone else. It's only about two weeks till you break up, isn't it?'

Katie nodded.

'Then you ought to let them know at once, before you go home this weekend.'

'Are you coming home this weekend?' asked Katie.

'Well, I was,' replied Ginny, 'but I'll leave the parents to you now. My news can wait until next weekend.'

'Your news? What's that? Come on, tell me.' Katie looked at Ginny with interest. 'What have you been up to?'

'Nothing. At least nothing that's my fault.' For a moment silence slipped between them and Katie forgot her own excitement to look speculatively at her sister. Ginny was staring down at the hearth rug, her face serious, her blue eyes unseeing. Now she looked at her more carefully, Katie noticed Ginny looked tired and pale. Worry had invaded her face and Katie was immediately concerned.

'What's the problem?' she asked softly. 'You're not still thinking of Roger, are you?'

Ginny looked up sharply. 'Of course not. That was over long ago, you know that.'

'I know it's over,' said Katie gently, 'but that doesn't necessarily mean *you* are over *it*.'

'Well, I am. I scarcely give him a thought these days.' Ginny smiled at her sister to take the sharpness from her words and went on, 'No, it's not man trouble at all. It's the agency. It's folded. I'm out of a job and, in the present economic climate, I've little chance of finding another.'

Katie was appalled. 'But Ginny, that's awful. What went wrong?'

Ginny shrugged. 'It's a competitive world, advertising,' she said. 'Too little work for too many companies. Actually, there was still work coming in, but they had a cash flow problem and in the end they couldn't pay their bills. They owe me quite a lot because they closed down without warning and without paying staff salaries.'

'Are you broke?' demanded Katie.

Ginny smiled at her sister's straight-forwardness. 'No,' she said. 'Not yet, but I'll have to go very carefully now.'

'Are you looking for another job?'

'Of course, but in the meantime I'll try to get some freelance work. Everyone's busy around Christmas, so I may be able to land something.'

'There must be hundreds of people looking for good art work,' said Katie, 'and yours is very good — strong yet sensitive. Surely you'll find something.'

Ginny looked into Katie's eyes, so full of consternation, and smiled reassuringly. 'I expect so. Don't worry. You're right — something's sure to turn up. You mustn't let it cloud your day, anyway. Tell me more about Don. I've only met him twice, you know.'

★   ★   ★

Two days later Ginny was sorting out her portfolio before starting on a dreary round of agencies and offices when the phone rang. It was Katie.

'Can I meet you for lunch?' she said. 'I've got to talk to you.'

Ginny laughed. 'You talked to me all Sunday night,' she said. 'Is there more to tell?'

Katie didn't laugh, however, but said, 'Something's come up which is quite important. Can you meet me at The

Ship at a quarter past twelve?'

Recognising that Katie was in a serious mood, Ginny agreed without further question.

Ginny arrived at The Ship, a pub a few minutes' walk from Katie's school, just before twelve-fifteen, but Katie was there before her, sitting at a table in the corner with drinks ready waiting. Ginny slid in beside her and accepted the tomato juice Katie pushed towards her.

'I've ordered us both cottage pie. Will that do?'

'Fine,' said Ginny. 'Now, what's the problem?'

The problem appeared to be Katie's holiday job. 'Mrs. Chilton was most upset when I went to see her yesterday,' Katie said. 'She said she didn't see why getting engaged should stop me from carrying on with the job as arranged. I pointed out that I wanted to spend Christmas with Don, but she wasn't very sympathetic. She said she didn't want to start looking for somebody else now.'

'Had you made the agreement in writing?' asked Ginny. 'If not, surely you can just say you've changed your mind.'

'I expect I could,' said Katie with a sigh, 'but, as she's a friend of Don's mother's, I don't want any bad feeling.'

'Does she know it's Don you're going to marry?'

'Yes, but we haven't told his mother yet, so I had to ask her not to say anything. That didn't help either. Then I thought of you.'

Ginny looked puzzled. 'Me? How can I help?'

'Take my place.'

'With Don?'

Katie gave a shout of laughter. 'No, idiot. In Austria.'

'What?' Ginny stared at her sister. 'I couldn't.'

'Why? Why couldn't you? You haven't a job and no commitments . . . '

'How do you know I've no commitments?' demanded Ginny, a spark of anger flashing at Katie's casual dismissal of her affairs.

'Well, have you?' challenged Katie, and Ginny had to admit she hadn't.

'Please, Ginny,' begged Katie. 'You'd be perfect, you'd love the skiing and the change would do you good.'

Their cottage pie arrived and neither girl pursued the conversation further while they ate their lunch, but both continued to give the idea thought. After her initial surprise at Katie's suggestion, Ginny didn't find the idea of taking her sister's place completely impossible. After all, sad though it was to admit it, she was an entirely free agent with nothing to hold her back. No man; no job. Katie was quite right when she said Ginny would enjoy the skiing — it was one of her favourite sports — but could she manage the children? No reason why not, really. There were only two of them, after all, and their grandmother would be there as well.

'What would the grandmother say?' she asked Katie at length.

'She says she won't hold me to an

agreement if you'll take my place.'

'You mean you've suggested me already?'

'I had to, Ginny. I was desperate. I couldn't not spend Christmas with Don, could I?' Katie's eyes were pleading, but a look of triumph lurked behind the plea, for Katie knew her sister well and knew that Ginny would come to her aid. Ginny had always rescued her from scrapes and escapades all their lives, and Katie knew that Ginny wouldn't let her down now.

'I'll have to meet her first,' began Ginny.

'Of course,' cried Katie. 'I said we'd be there at about half-past four. Can you meet me from school at a quarter to?'

Ginny gave up being annoyed and laughed ruefully. 'You mean you've fixed it up already? Supposing I'd said no.'

'Oh, I knew you wouldn't,' said Katie delightedly. 'I knew I could rely on you. You're the best sister in the world. You won't regret it, I promise you.'

But Ginny was already beginning to regret it. She'd allowed herself to be hustled into a decision she might have preferred to delay and, when Katie disappeared back to her classroom for the afternoon, Ginny walked alone through the cold winter streets wondering what she had let herself in for. Well, at least it was only for three weeks and, though she would miss Christmas at home in Somerset with her parents, she would enjoy the skiing.

★   ★   ★

Mrs. Chilton lived in a mews cottage in Knightsbridge. It was obviously loved and cared for, and had window boxes on the sills and a gleaming brass knocker on the front door.

The old lady herself came in answer to Katie's knock, and greeted both girls with a smile. She led the way into a small drawing-room with windows at each end, one looking out on to the mews and the other, an attractive bow window, giving on to a tiny paved courtyard garden at the back of the house.

Mrs. Chilton waved them to a sofa beside the fireplace and resumed her own seat opposite them.

'Sit down and be comfortable,' she said. 'It's a bitter day outside.'

Katie introduced her sister to Mrs. Chilton and they all chatted for a moment, while the two girls held out cold fingers to the fire.

'Would you like some tea?' asked Mrs. Chilton. 'Mrs. Merton, my help, has gone home, but she always leaves a trolley laid for me in the kitchen. I'm not very good with trays — ' she held out her arthritic hands with a rueful smile — 'but I can manage the trolley.'

'That would be lovely,' cried Katie, jumping to her feet. 'Shall I go and make it? I can easily find the extra cups.'

'That would be very kind, my dear,' said Mrs. Chilton.

Katie disappeared into the kitchen, leaving Ginny to sit with Mrs. Chilton. Mrs. Chilton didn't waste any further time on idle chatter, but looked across at Ginny, studying her for a moment. She liked what she saw; a sensible well-dressed young woman with a minimum of cleverly applied make-up. Her blue eyes were candid and friendly, and her smile enlivened her face so that one hardly noticed that her mouth was a fraction too large and her chin too determined. The whole was framed by a mass of fair curls, a little unruly, but none the less attractive for that. Mrs. Chilton found her frank appraisal was returned, and she said easily. 'I understand you're prepared to take your sister's place as my help when I take my grandchildren to Austria.'

Ginny smiled. 'I will, if you are agreeable,' she said, 'but I'm not a trained teacher like Katie, so I've only general experience with children.'

'That needn't necessarily worry us,' replied Mrs. Chilton. 'Common sense and a willingness to join in with the family are what I'm looking for; another pair of hands in the rush hour, so to speak.' She laughed and added, 'You should have time for skiing yourself while the children are in ski school. Or, to do anything else — painting, for instance. I gather you're an artist.'

'A commercial artist, yes, though I paint for my own pleasure, too, of course.'

'Harriet draws quite well — that's my granddaughter. She's only seven but some of her pictures are really very good.'

'What's the little boy's name?' Ginny asked.

'David,' replied his grandmother, 'but he's not so little. He's ten and big for his age. He's keen on all sports and games and is good at them, too.'

'He should enjoy the skiing, then,' said Ginny.

'Oh, he will,' said Mrs. Chilton. 'He's been before and soon found his feet. When Caroline and Peter took him last time — ' she paused a moment and then said softly — 'you heard about my daughter and son-in-law?'

'Yes,' replied Ginny gently. 'I'm so very sorry.'

The old lady nodded and then, with a conscious effort, pulled herself together and went on, 'When they took David last time, Caroline said he had no fear at all, he just followed his instructor, never really assuming he might not be able to do it.'

'But Harriet hasn't skied before?'

'No, she was too young last time. But I expect she'll enjoy it. She's always very keen to do what David does. Are you a good skier like Katie?'

'Far better,' said Katie, appearing at the door, pushing a laden trolley in front of her. 'Your Mrs. Merton has done us proud. Look at all this.'

She wheeled the trolley over to Mrs. Chilton's chair while Ginny rose and closed the door behind her. Mrs. Chilton poured the tea, a little shakily, and invited the girls to help themselves to sandwiches, biscuits and cakes.

When they were comfortably settled once more, Mrs. Chilton went on, 'Gareth, my son, has arranged for us to stay in a house in the village. I gather it's run by a widow who likes to take in families on holiday rather than couples or individuals. Some friends of ours stayed there last year. They say she's very good — takes care of the cooking, washing and all that side of things — gives one a real holiday.'

Ginny agreed, wondering privately how much cooking and washing Mrs. Chilton did when she wasn't on holiday.

'Will you be the only family staying in the house?' asked Katie.

'Yes,' answered Mrs. Chilton. 'This woman — I can't remember her name — only takes one family at a time. She likes her house to remain a home even if she has to share it. More tea, Ginny?'

'Thank you.' Ginny passed her cup. 'Will I be able to meet the children before we go?' she asked.

'I'm not sure,' replied Mrs. Chilton. 'They've been staying with their other grandparents in Yorkshire since the accident and they're only coming here the night before we go.'

'Will they live in Yorkshire permanently?' asked Katie.

'No, that's only temporary. Gareth, my son, is going to move into a bigger house and the children will go there in the holidays. During the term they're going to go to boarding school.'

Ginny was surprised at this. 'Aren't they a bit young to board?' she asked.

Mrs. Chilton's smile did not alter exactly, but it seemed to freeze on her face. 'We have a difficult set of circumstances which need to be reconciled or overcome,' she said tightly. 'You must let us be the best judge of our children's future.'

'Oh, of course,' said Ginny hastily. 'I didn't mean to criticise.'

'I'm sure you didn't, my dear,' agreed Mrs. Chilton smoothly.

Darkness had fallen by the time they left the mews cottage, and with it had come a steady drizzle.

'I'm meeting Don for a bite of supper,' said Katie. 'Are you going to come?'

Ginny shook her head. 'No, thanks,' she said. 'I'll see Don to give him my congratulations another time. I've got an interview with another agency tomorrow and I have some more work to sort through.'

'Right, well, I'll see you soon,' said Katie cheerfully. 'Next weekend at home, if not before.' She gave her sister a hug and, flagging down a passing taxi, jumped in and was driven away through the traffic to meet Don.

★ ★ ★

The days before her departure for Austria were busy ones for Ginny. She presented her portfolio to several advertising agencies and, though they showed a sympathetic interest, none of them offered her work, either permanent or freelance. They filed her name and address and photostats of a selection of her work, promising to phone should a job suitable to her particular talents come in, but they never sounded very optimistic and neither was she. She spent several days doing her Christmas shopping, so that all her presents for the family and friends were wrapped and ready to be delivered before she left, and she added a doll for Harriet, a pocket chess set for David and some soap for Mrs. Chilton to take with her.

She spent the last weekend in Somerset visiting her parents, with whom she exchanged parcels, and then, loaded with ski suit, boots and skis, she wished them an early Happy Christmas and was driven back to London by Katie and Don, who had also been visiting.

Packed and ready, she indulged in the luxury of a taxi to take her and her luggage to the mews cottage. It wasn't really an extravagance, she decided. Coping with skis and a suitcase on the

Tube would be very awkward and, anyway, she was being paid from today.

A young girl answered to her knock, only opening the door a little and peering round it. She had wide blue eyes which solemnly regarded Ginny, and her hair, the colour of dark corn, was tied back in a pony tail, leaving a little elfin face with a pointed chin unframed and strangely vulnerable.

Ginny said, 'Hello, you must be Harriet.' The girl nodded but didn't speak or move to open the door further, so Ginny went on, 'I'm Ginny. I'm coming on holiday with you.'

The child eyed her for a moment or two longer and then said, 'Come in. Granny's in there.' She opened the door wider to let Ginny step inside, nodding towards the drawing-room as she did so.

Ginny carried her case and skis into the narrow hallway, looking round for somewhere to put them where they would be out of the way. She could hear Mrs. Chilton speaking to someone and, as she turned to follow Harriet into the drawing-room, a man peered over the banisters and called, 'Harri, who was at the door?'

To which Harriet called back, 'The helping girl who's coming with us.'

The man looked at Ginny for a moment and then came round the end of the banister and descended the stairs. When he reached the bottom, he stared at her, his face registering mild surprise. Ginny's prepared greeting died on her lips as he looked her over, for all the world, thought Ginny, as if she were a prize heifer. She had no doubt as to who he was and, as Katie's description of him came back to her, she felt herself smiling.

'You're not the girl I engaged,' he said at last.

'No,' agreed Ginny, far more calmly than she felt, as the flicker of amusement she had known on recognising Gareth Chilton from Katie's description fled before anger at his rudeness. 'I'm her sister, Virginia. How do you do?' She half-extended her hand but, as he ignored the movement, she let it fall to her side again.

'And where is she? Katie, I mean. Why have you come instead?'

'Because I arranged it with her,' said a voice at Ginny's side. 'Don't bully her, Gareth.'

'I'm not bullying anyone, Mother. But I think you might have told me about the change of plans. I am the children's guardian after all.'

'And I'm their grandmother. Don't be so prickly, Gareth. Ginny is an admirable substitute for Katie. After all, so long as I have someone sensible on hand to help, it doesn't matter who it is, does it?'

Gareth looked as if he might say more but, obviously loth to argue with his mother in front of the cause of that argument, he bit back the words and stood frowning.

Mrs. Chilton turned to Ginny. 'So nice to see you again, my dear.'

Ginny ignored Gareth's glare and

said warmly, 'I've been looking forward to it. I thought I might be able to give a hand with last-minute packing.'

'What a kind thought, my dear, but I think Gareth and Mrs. Merton have everything in hand.' Harriet had been standing aloof from the goings-on around her, watching in silence. Now she slipped her hand into her grandmother's and Mrs. Chilton pulled her forward gently. 'And this is Harriet,' she said. 'Harriet, this is Ginny.'

Harriet nodded, but said nothing.

'We met at the door,' said Ginny smiling at the little girl.

'And here's David.'

David had come down the stairs and was peering round his uncle, who was still standing on the bottom step.

'Hello,' he said cheerfully. 'Can you ski?'

'Yes,' said Ginny.

'Are you good?'

Ginny grinned. 'I can get down a hill,' she said. 'What about you?'

'I can get down a hill,' he said

echoing her casual tone. 'I say, are those your skis?' He pointed to the skis in their canvas cover standing in the corner. 'I wish I had my own skis.'

He looked hopefully at his grandmother who said, 'There's absolutely no point until you've stopped growing.'

David pulled a face at this and said, 'But hired skis are never much good.'

'Don't be silly, David,' said Gareth sharply and then added, to soften his words, 'no doubt Ginny will help you choose yours.'

'Yes, we'll soon sort you out,' said Ginny. 'Both of you,' she added with a glance at Harriet who was still clutching her grandmother's hand.

'Then we're all sure to have lots of fun.' Mrs. Chilton took charge. 'Is that your luggage, Ginny? Good, leave it there. Gareth'll be bringing the rest down in a little while. Are you ready up there, Gareth?'

'Very nearly, Mother. Don't worry — you've got plenty of time. Aren't you going to eat something before you go?'

'Yes, yes. Mrs. Merton has made soup and sandwiches for us all. As soon as you've brought the luggage down we'll eat.'

'Right.' Gareth went back upstairs, taking David with him.

There was little conversation while they ate except between Gareth and his mother.

Mrs. Chilton's apparent frailty concealed a determined nature, and her strength of character was reflected in her son. After his initial annoyance at Ginny's appearance in place of her sister, he treated her courteously enough when he spoke to her. Nevertheless, there was little warmth in his attitude and she felt he disapproved of her. At the back of her mind she could hear Katie's wry comment: 'Probably thinks he's God's gift to women', and she couldn't help agreeing with it. It was with some relief that she rose from the table and the whole party prepared to load Gareth's car and drive to the airport.

Ginny sat in the back of the car with a child on either side of her. David chattered cheerfully but Harriet remained silent, almost withdrawn, and Ginny noticed that the little girl kept her eyes tightly shut all the way down the motorway to Heathrow. Of course, her parents had been killed in a motorway pile-up. Very gently, and without saying anything, Ginny placed her hand over Harriet's. For a moment there was no reaction and then the little girl's fingers twisted and clutched at Ginny's, holding them in an iron grip until Gareth turned off the motorway and drove through the tunnel into the airport.

He helped them check their baggage through and then he said, 'I won't wait, Mother. Your flight won't be called for nearly an hour yet.'

He gave her a quick hug and then turned to the children. 'Have a lovely time,' he said, bending down to take Harriet in his arms for a moment. 'Help Granny and Ginny all you can, won't you? And I'll be with you on Christmas

Eve so you'll be able to show me how well you can ski.'

'Will you ski with us, Uncle Gareth?' demanded David.

'Of course I will,' promised his uncle.

Ginny listened to the conversation in amazement. She had had no idea Gareth was to join them in Austria, and she wasn't at all sure she liked the idea.

Something of her thoughts must have shown on her face, for when Gareth turned to her to say goodbye, he smiled sardonically and said, 'You didn't realise I'd be joining you? Well, never mind, now you've something to look forward to.' Before she could think of a fitting reply, he had turned from her again and, amidst a chorus of goodbyes, he had disappeared into the crowds.

2

The journey was comparatively easy, and the children's excitement carried them through it. Once they were on the aeroplane, Harriet unfroze a little. It seemed that she had no fear of flying and, as soon as she had left the car, a touch of colour returned to her pale little face. By the time they were aboard the aircraft, she was arguing with David as to who should have the window seat, and Ginny knew that, for a while at least, the child's fear had departed.

There was a car journey the other end to take them from the airport to St. Georg-im-Wald, but the novelty of being in a left-hand drive car and on the 'wrong' side of the road seemed to alter things, and Harriet showed no signs of being afraid. She kept her nose pressed to the window and called excitedly to David as they passed through unknown country — forests of tall and silent firs, villages whose houses huddled round churches topped with pointed spires or onion towers; and all nestling under a blanket of snow. Above and beyond them were the mountains, magnificent peaks capped with white and, as they travelled across the valley floor, they seemed enclosed by the mountain walls on every side. Darkness fell, and the bright lights of the shops and houses they passed looked warm and inviting. As they left each town and returned to the darkness enfolding it, the car's headlamps cut swathes of light gleaming on the snow banked up beside the road.

Gradually, they left the valley floor and began toiling up the mountain road which led to villages higher up the slopes. The way was steep and twisting and the driver of the car seemed to keep his hand permanently on the horn.

At last, after what seemed to be ages without passing through a village, they swung round a jutting rock and emerged unexpectedly into a village square. Dominated on one side by a large hotel proclaiming itself the Hotel Eidelweiss, the square was enclosed by smaller guest houses and shops, with narrow roads twisting away between them to other houses, shops and bars less centrally positioned.

The driver took one of these and wound his way up a narrow lane past the church to a small house set in a tiny garden. On the front wall of the house was a beautiful mural of alpine flowers and the words *Haus Elisabeth* in flowing script.

Tired and hungry, the party tumbled out of the car and, on instruction from Mrs. Chilton, Ginny went to the front door to ring the bell while she supervised the driver unloading the baggage. Before Ginny could reach the door, however, it was flung wide in welcome and a dumpy woman rushed out to greet her.

'*Wilkommen! Wilkommen!* English family to the Haus Elisabeth.' She grasped Ginny by the hand before hurrying on to meet the children and Mrs. Chilton.

The warmth of the house enfolded them like a blanket. They hadn't been cold in the car, but the night air was freezing and they were glad to be indoors.

Their hostess closed the door behind the departing driver and said, 'I am named Elisabeth. Here is my house.'

Mrs. Chilton introduced them all and Elisabeth beamed again at everyone. Harriet yawned suddenly and Elisabeth, who had been about to show them over the house, cried, 'Ah! The little one is tired. I have food prepared. You must eat and then sleep, *ja*?'

Two hours later, with the children warm, fed and fast asleep in bed, Ginny snuggled down under her own feather bed. She looked forward to seeing the village by daylight and to exploring the surrounding mountains.

★   ★   ★

Next morning she flung wide her shutters to discover a crisply brilliant day. The sky was clear ice blue and the mountain peaks were sharply defined against it. She opened the window and leant out to enjoy the view. The cold air made her gasp as she drew it down into her lungs, but it gave her a thrill of excitement; gone for the moment were her worries about having no job and no prospects of one. She felt vital and alive and determined to enjoy the reality of the moment. The future, grey and uncertain, was relegated to the back of her mind and, suddenly incredibly hungry, she turned back into her room to dress for breakfast.

She was almost ready when her door flew open and David and Harriet bounded in, still wearing their pyjamas.

'What clothes shall we wear?'

'Are we going skiing?'

Their questions came tumbling without pause for answer, and Ginny laughed as she tried to cope with them all. She suggested they put on their salopettes and offered to help Harriet with hers.

'I can do it,' cried Harriet indignantly. Ginny waited on the landing while the children threw their clothes on, calling to her from their room all the time.

Elisabeth heard them coming and was soon bustling through with hot chocolate for the children and coffee for Ginny. The rolls on the table were crusty and fresh, and they all tucked in with enthusiasm.

Mrs. Chilton appeared as the others were about to leave the table. 'Now, tell me everyone's plans,' she said, sitting down and pouring herself some coffee. There was a chorus of suggestions from the children, but Mrs. Chilton hushed them and addressed herself to Ginny.

'What do you think, my dear?'

'Well, we must hire skis and boots first,' she replied.

'Of course. Elisabeth will tell you where.'

'Then I thought the children should enrol for ski school.'

There was immediate protest from David. 'Oh, not ski school. I don't need lessons. I can ski already.'

'I'm sure you can,' agreed Ginny, 'but you won't know your way around, and if you go with a class you'll learn the best runs.'

'Are you going into ski school?' he demanded.

'I don't know. I might take some lessons in case I'm a bit rusty, but it'll be in a different class because I've been skiing longer than you.'

'I wanted to ski with you!' David complained.

'And so you shall,' said Ginny. 'Lessons will probably break between twelve and half-past one. We can eat a quick lunch and then ski together until classes start again.'

'That's not long,' grumbled David.

'And we can ski after lessons until the lifts stop,' added Ginny. 'Besides,' she went on, 'you want to have improved by the time Uncle Gareth gets here, don't you? He promised he'd ski with you, and you'll want to be able to keep up with him.'

'I suppose so,' said David, still unconvinced.

*   *   *

Following directions from Elisabeth, they were soon at Franz Meyer's ski shop and the children were fitted with boots and skis. From there they moved on to the ski school and bought lesson tickets, and then they followed the sign to the ski school meeting place at the bottom of a small draglift. Ginny spoke to the director, who pointed out a children's beginner class for Harriet and carried David off to a more advanced class.

'You are a good skier, *ja?*' he enquired.

'Oh, yes,' answered David confidently.

The man smiled. 'Very good. You go with Fritz.' And so David joined a group of children much his own age, waiting with a cheerful young man of about nineteen.

Ginny waited with Harriet until her teacher, Hannah, arrived and, with both children safely provided for, she collected her own skis.

The lift queues caused by the ski classes being taken up the mountain had disappeared by the time Ginny was ready to go, and so she got on to the chair-lift after only a moment's wait. As she swung gently above the snow-covered mountain, she had a breath-taking view down through the peaks to the valley floor several thousand feet below; and yet she herself was far below the crests still towering above her.

Immediately beneath her, was the village itself and, by using the church as a guide, she managed to pinpoint *Haus Elisabeth* before the chairs began passing through a dense forest of firs, utterly still and burdened with several inches of snow.

Voices of skiers on the woodland trails, or calling from one chair to another, carried on the pellucid air, but they didn't disturb the silence which enfolded Ginny.

When the chairlift emerged from the firs, Ginny found herself approaching the lift station, set in the middle of a bowl in the hills. She was now above the tree line, and prepared *pistes* marked with coloured markers to denote their difficulty stretched away on all sides. Further over, she could see another chair, a double one this time, carrying skiers to a peak on the extreme edge of the bowl.

As soon as she had got off the chair, Ginny crossed over to the huge map on the wall of the lift station. For a small village, St. Georg boasted a great deal of skiing, and Ginny discovered it linked with another village, Gruneberg, on the far side of one of the peaks. In fact, if she took the second, double chairlift further over, she could decide, on reaching the top, whether to ski down this side back to St. Georg or down the other to Gruneberg.

At the top of the second chair, there was a little chalet restaurant, and Ginny made a mental note that it might be fun to take the children there for lunch one day.

Now, however she decided to test her legs on a simple run, and headed for one of the shorter draglifts. She hadn't all that much time anyway because she had promised Harriet faithfully that she would be waiting at the ski-school meeting place at twelve, when her class finished. One of the runs from the top of her chosen draglift was a red, medium run and, as Ginny set off down it, she found to her delight that her skis responded and she could negotiate the slope without problem.

Halfway down she saw a children's class lined up watching, as their instructor demonstrated simple parallel turns. Recognising David's blue and red ski suit, Ginny paused to watch. David hadn't seen her, and when it was his turn to attempt the turns he managed them very creditably.

'Bend a lot,' called the instructor, 'and it will be good.'

David turned and began side-stepping up the hill to join the end of the line. Ginny skied over to him and, at the sound of her skis, he looked up and grinned. 'Hello,' he called. 'Did you see that? I did them without falling.'

'Yes, I did see. Well done. Have you got a nice instructor?'

'He's all right,' said David, 'but I like going faster than this.'

Ginny smiled sympathetically. 'Never mind,' she said. 'We'll have a go after lunch, without stopping to do exercises.'

'Great,' said David. 'See you at the bottom.'

'See you,' said Ginny, accepting her dismissal and, with an easy turn, she skied non-stop to the top of the first chairlift — the middle station. The skiing wasn't difficult, but she wasn't as fit as she should be. Normally Ginny would have prepared herself for her holiday by doing ski exercises, but because she had come at such short notice she had done none. Already her calves and thighs were aching and she knew by the next morning she would be stiff everywhere. Still, she'd come to ski and ski she would.

She spent the next three quarters of an hour playing on the easy slopes served by the short draglifts, and then set off down the woodland trail leading back to the village. It was further than she had thought, for the trail curved right through the woods, crossing beneath the chairlift several times before emerging on to a smooth steep snowfield above the village, which in turn gave way to the gentle nursery slopes where Harriet would be. As she paused on the edge of the wood, a man swept past her at a tremendous speed, his skis hissing over the snow and, on reaching the edge of the steep snowfield, he crouched in the *schuss* position, tucked his poles under his arms and headed straight down to the village.

Ginny watched him enviously, wishing she skied with such style, and then set off after him, following his trail as closely as she could. Her confidence had grown during the morning and as she sped over the snow, gathering speed on the steep slope, she felt exhilarated. There was nothing in her mind but elation edged with fear at her meteoric descent and, when she finally *schussed* to a stop above the nursery slope, she was laughing aloud at her own excitement.

She paused again to catch her breath, and then looked across at the various groups spread out on the nursery slopes. She spotted Harriet's class quickly, and watched from a distance to see how the little girl was doing.

With the resilience and determination of most seven-year-old skiers, Harriet was side-stepping up a little slope and then in her turn trying to snow plough down it, her legs so widespread that her bottom nearly touched the ground. Ginny watched her fall and pick herself up again to struggle on and fall once more. The other children were doing the same, and Harriet's instructor, a young woman of infinite patience, was picking them up, dusting them off and encouraging them all.

* * *

When classes finished at lunchtime, Ginny walked the children back to *Haus Elisabeth* for lunch. Over the meal, which was taken quickly to allow David to drag Ginny on to the slopes once more, the children vied with each other in their accounts of their morning.

'I'll walk Harriet up to ski school at one-thirty,' offered Mrs. Chilton, 'so you and David can go off now and Harriet doesn't have to wait around in the cold.'

Ginny was impressed with the way David skied. He had no fear of falling and tended to take the most direct

47

route down the hillside, turning only when absolutely necessary. Several times he did fall, and twice the bindings on his skis broke open to release his foot as he fell awkwardly. Ginny, putting him back together again, was pleased that they did; it reassured her to know that they were properly adjusted, so that should he take a bad tumble, his skis would come off and his legs wouldn't get twisted or broken.

They spent all afternoon on the mountain, the children back with their classes and Ginny exploring further afield alone, and then, when the lifts closed and darkness crept up from the valley, they went home for hot chocolate and delicious cream cakes to keep them going until supper.

Elisabeth served an evening meal at seven, so to pass the time, the children dragged Ginny to the indoor swimming pool attached to the Eidelweiss Hotel.

By the time she got them into bed they were both exhausted and slept almost instantly, and Ginny herself was ready to doze over her book by the fireside.

* * *

That first day set the tenor of successive ones. David was delighted with his ski class; his instructor kept the repetitive exercises to a minimum and took the children all over the mountain so that, by the end of the week, there wasn't a run blue, red or black that David hadn't tackled. The blacks were negotiated very carefully, and all the children were warned not to try them on their own, but the range of skiing had done wonders for David's confidence and he was longing for Gareth to arrive so he could demonstrate his ability.

Harriet got on well, too, and progressed to some of the blue runs higher up the mountain. She couldn't ski back down to the village, but after lessons in the afternoon she and Ginny would ski the blues happily and then come down to the village on the chair ready to meet David and go swimming.

When the evening meal was over and the children were in bed, Ginny and Mrs. Chilton sat beside the fire and drank their coffee in peace. Their conversation ranged comfortably from topic to topic with the ease of old friends.

On the third or fourth day, Mrs. Chilton said, 'You must feel free to go out in the evenings, Ginny. You don't have to stay in and sit with me, you know.'

Ginny smiled. 'Thank you,' she answered, 'but I'm quite happy by the fire.'

'Well, if you make any friends up on the hill,' said Mrs. Chilton, 'and they ask you to join them later, please do. I shan't be going out, so there'll be no baby-sitting problems.'

Ginny thanked her again and said she would remember. In fact, she had met a couple on the hill that very morning, Mary and John Lancer, and had skied with them for the rest of the day. She had enjoyed the day immensely but had refused their offer to join them for tea afterwards because she was taking the children swimming. However, they had arranged to meet again next morning when David and Harriet were safely in ski school, and Ginny was looking forward to it.

She wasn't looking forward so much to Gareth's arrival in two days' time. During their fireside conversations, Mrs. Chilton had often spoken of her son and Ginny learnt a good deal more about him; what a good businessman he was, a director of several companies, what a thoughtful son, what a generous uncle to the children. Mrs. Chilton praised him to the sky, and at times Ginny felt awkward. Her own fleeting impression of Gareth made it seem as though they must be talking of a different man. Mrs. Chilton bemoaned the fact that he wasn't married, though he had lots of girl friends.

'I bet he has,' thought Ginny, and decided that anyone who did end up married to that paragon, Gareth Chilton, would have a lot to live up to in the eyes of her mother-in-law.

★ ★ ★

Christmas eve arrived at last, and the children positively bubbled with excitement. Not only was the *Haus Elisabeth* being decorated by a beaming Elisabeth, but it was the day that Uncle Gareth was due to arrive.

'Will he ski with us today?' cried David as he prepared to join his ski class.

'I doubt it,' laughed Ginny struggling with a clip on Harriet's boots. 'He won't be here till it's dark, I don't expect.'

'I can't wait! I can't wait!' squeaked Harriet, wriggling her feet in anticipation and making Ginny's job more difficult.

'Well, I'm afraid you'll have to,' said Ginny. 'Keep still a minute while I fix this clip. The best way to make the day go quickly is to keep busy. I tell you what, I'll meet you both at twelve and we'll go up to the restaurant at the top of the double chair and have lunch there.'

There were cries of delight at this suggestion and, still effervescent, the children joined their classes for the morning. It turned out that there were no classes in the afternoon. The ski school closed at noon to allow time for the Christmas Eve preparations.

'You see,' Elisabeth had explained earlier, 'in Austria the presents are exchanged on Christmas Eve.'

After their mountain-top lunch, Ginny brought them down to the middle station on the chairlift, and then very slowly and carefully helped Harriet to take the long winding woodland trail back down to the village. The little girl conscientiously followed Ginny's instructions and, to David's irriation, they paused regularly to catch their breath and for Ginny to encourage Harriet.

But Harriet needed little encouragement; she had faith in Ginny and, by following her, managed the whole trail without falling.

When they reached the open snow-fields above the village, David disappeared down the hill at high speed and Ginny said, 'Now, you lead the way and I'll follow. There's plenty of room, so make nice wide turns.'

Harriet set off and, gaining in confidence and speed, came down the last slope in fine style. Ginny followed her, ready to pick her up if disaster struck, but the little girl went well, her legs fixed in the snow plough position, completely in control of her descent.

David was waiting at the bottom, and with him stood a tall man. Both were watching Harriet. At first Ginny thought David was with John Lancer, but as she drew nearer she saw with surprise that it was Gareth Chilton, dressed in his ski suit, his skis on his feet.

Harriet recognised him too. Squealing with delight, she careered towards him and, with arms wide, used him as a buffer to stop herself. He swung her up into the air and gave her a bear-like hug.

'Fantastic, Harriet,' he said. 'You were going like a train. Good girl.'

'I didn't fall once,' cried the delighted Harriet as Gareth set her down.

'Well done, well done,' he said. 'I saw David coming down like the clappers, but I didn't expect to see you following him.'

Ginny skied up beside them and Gareth grinned at her. 'Hello,' he said. 'Having fun?'

'Hello. We didn't expect you until later.' The words came out rather abruptly and she felt awkward. Unwanted colour flooded her cheeks and she said quickly, 'Didn't Harriet come down well?'

Gareth looked amused by her blush and said, 'She did indeed. Well, are we going up again?'

With cries of 'Oh, yes,' the children turned immediately for the chairlift and, with a burst of exuberance, Gareth raced David for a place in the queue.

They managed several more runs before the lifts closed and they finished for the day. Ginny was impressed with the way Gareth skied, smoothly and effortlessly hissing over the snow.

★   ★   ★

Dusk came creeping up the hillside and, as they reached the bottom for the last time, the lights from the village gleamed brightly to greet them. St. Georg was preparing for Christmas and the four of them quickly caught the mood.

When they reached Haus Elisabeth, Mrs. Chilton was waiting for them. The children bounded in full of their skiing exploits and their excitement at finding Uncle Gareth waiting for them.

At last, when their grandmother was able to make herself heard, she said, 'Now, baths and change, please, and everyone downstairs in an hour.' She turned to Ginny and said, 'I'll deal with the children. You carry on and get yourself ready — we've Christmas dinner tonight.'

Ginny went into her own room and flopped on to her bed. Elisabeth had told them that morning that Christmas dinner would be tonight, and they had decided to give the children their presents then. Ginny was thoughtful now. She had bought her presents at home and then discovered later that Gareth would be there, too. Ought she to have something for him? She had considered the matter for several days and at length decided to get something small — a mere token — so that if he gave her something she would have a present for him in return, and if not she would simply keep it in her bag. She had been into the shops in the village and bought a small wood carving. It was a squirrel, delicately wrought, poised on the top of a tree stump as if about to leap away. It cost more than the token she had had in mind but she could see nothing else to buy him; and if in the end she didn't give it to

Gareth, she could keep it herself as a souvenir of her holiday. As she lay on her bed, she glanced at the pile of presents stacked neatly on the chest of drawers and wondered whether to give Gareth the squirrel anyway.

She was still undecided when she had showered and changed into a warm sweater dress of dusky pink. Its cowl neckline flattered her shoulders, and its soft folds clung gently to display her slim figure to great advantage. The warmth of its colour brought a glow to her cheeks and, when she gave herself a last glance in the mirror, she was pleased with her appearance.

There was a loud bang on her door. 'Ginny!' called Harriet. 'Are you ready? We're all going down.'

'I'm ready,' she called and, scooping up all the presents, including the squirrel, she opened the door and joined the family on the landing.

As they came down the stairs, Elisabeth emerged from her end of the house and, with a conspiratorial smile on her face and a finger on her lips, she led the children into the living-room. The adults held back for a moment to watch the children's faces when they saw the room. Both of them paused on the threshold, and Harriet's eyes shone with wonder as she saw how the room had been transformed. 'It's beautiful,' she breathed and, stepping on tiptoe as if she feared to disturb it, she crept forward to look.

The room was lit entirely by candles, some set amongst the decorative greenery, others in sconces on shelves and tables. In one corner was a Christmas tree whose tinsel and trimmings reflected the light of its own candles to shimmer and gleam, and in another was a crib. Tall carved wooden figures depicted the stable scene, with angels and shepherds, kings and animals, and, of course, Joseph and Mary. The manger, straw-lined, waited for the baby to be placed there on Christmas Day.

Harriet knelt beside the crib and

stared at it for a long moment, then quietly crossed over to Gareth and said, her voice breaking in a sob, 'It's so beautiful. I wish my mummy could see it.'

Gareth gathered her into his arms and rocked her gently, his face against her hair, and said, 'So do I, sweetheart, so do I.'

For a moment there was silence as all four remembered their loss, and Ginny saw tears gleaming in everyone's eyes. She felt them prick her own, and wished there was something she could do to ease the children's pain. She felt she was intruding and longed to slip away, but she was too far from the door to retreat unobserved.

It was Elisabeth who eased the moment. She knew the situation, because Mrs. Chilton had explained so that no unwitting comment about parents was made. Now she saw the tears and recognised the grief and very quietly turned on the lamps so that the spell of the candlelight was broken.

'Look at all the presents under the tree,' she said softly, and the children's eyes were immediately turned in that direction. Ginny, still holding her own pile of presents, moved across to the tree and added them to those already there. She sat back on her heels and said, 'There. Now there are even more.'

★　★　★

The evening was a merry one, despite the underlying sadness which showed itself from time to time. In a moment's quiet while both children were struggling to unwrap their last and biggest gifts, Gareth appeared at Ginny's side.

'Thank you for my squirrel, he's beautiful.'

Ginny smiled. 'I'm glad you like him. I did, too. Thank you for my perfume — it's one of my favourites.' The package was still in her hand and she held it up as she spoke.

'Sorry it wasn't gift wrapped,' apologised Gareth with a grin, as he saw again the duty-free shop paper. 'I'm not much of a hand at wrapping.'

'You seem to have made a good job of those,' said Ginny, nodding at the parcels which still defied the children. 'They are from you, I suppose.'

'Oh, the shop did those, they — ' He was interrupted by a cry of delight from David who had at last unwrapped his present. There, lying revealed in all their glory, was a pair of skis, complete with shining bindings. He flung himself at his uncle, pouring out his thanks. Harriet, longing to know what her enormous parcel contained, ripped at the paper with renewed vigour and at last discovered a toboggan, gleaming wood with steel runners, painted bright red. With a squeal of joy, she cast herself into Gareth's arms, hugging and kissing him so that he almost had to fend her off.

'They really are marvellous presents,' Ginny murmured to Gareth.

Gareth smiled sadly. 'I'm glad they were so satisfactory. I wanted them to have something really special, because — well, you know why.' He turned away and Ginny knew his own grief was very near the surface.

The evening remained cheerful, however. Gareth managed to keep the party bright without it seeming an effort, and suddenly Ginny was glad she had left the squirrel in with the other presents; quite apart from the fact that she had received a gift from him, the giving pleased her. She had warmed to Gareth for the way he entertained the children, involving them in games and songs so that there was no time to dwell on the fact that Caroline and Peter Croyd were not with them.

At last he piggy-backed the children upstairs and, worn out from a day's skiing, an evening's partying and a huge Christmas meal, both children tumbled into bed to sleep the sleep of exhaustion until the morning. He came back downstairs and, collapsing into an armchair, said, 'Are you going to the service, Mother?'

His mother shook her head. 'No, I don't think so, dear. I think I'll just go on up to bed.' Suddenly she looked very tired and old and Ginny longed to be able to help her in some way. But Mrs. Chilton was a woman of character, and with Gareth's aid she got to her feet. With dry bright eyes she turned to Ginny, a look of gratitude on her face.

'Good night, my dear. Thank you for helping to make this evening so happy. As you can imagine, it wasn't an easy one for any of us.'

Impulsively, Ginny leaned forward and kissed the old lady on the cheek. 'Thank you for letting me share it.'

Mrs. Chilton smiled. 'Now don't come up, Gareth. I'm perfectly able to take myself upstairs.' She kissed her son good night and went up alone.

Gareth turned back into the room. 'I must add my thanks to Mother's,' he said. The strain of the evening had told on him, too, and he poured himself a brandy from a bottle on the sideboard. He held the glass out to Ginny, but she shook her head.

'No, thanks,' she said. 'Not for me.' He sat down with his drink and there was a brief silence before she said, 'Are you going to the service?'

Gareth glanced up at her. 'Yes, I think so. Elisabeth says that an English clergyman holds a midnight service in a room at the Hotel Eidelweiss.'

'May I come with you?'

'Of course. I'd be pleased if you did.'

A few minutes before twelve, they stepped out into the cold night to walk to the Eidelweiss. Gareth took Ginny's arm and they walked together in silence, their feet crunching on the icy pavements and, as Christmas Eve slipped into Christmas Day, they joined a small congregation of English tourists in welcoming the Christ-child. Ginny knew she would never forget this evening — nor the strong, compassionate man who stood beside her.

★   ★   ★

Despite their late night, the children were awake early on Christmas morning, bursting with excitement. David's new skis and Harriet's toboggan were standing side by side in the hall, and both children were longing to try them out on the slopes.

St. Georg, catering for its tourists, ran the lifts on Christmas Day, though the ski school was closed, so they had not got long to wait.

As soon as breakfast was finished, Gareth took David with his new skis and his boots to the ski shop to have the safety bindings adjusted, while Ginny helped Harriet to get ready for a morning on the hill.

Harriet had decided to take both toboggan and skis to the mountain so that when she got tired of one pastime she could change to the other.

A pale sun was fighting its way through a layer of cloud as Ginny and Harriet walked up to the nursery slopes, carrying skis and dragging the new toboggan behind them. The village was surprisingly busy. Many of the shops were open and there was a queue at the bottom of the chairlift. As they reached the meeting place at the foot of the nursery slopes, David called out, waving them to come over.

'We're going right to the top,' David cried as Ginny and Harriet approached.

'That sounds fantastic,' laughed Ginny. 'Those skis look good, you'll go like the wind on those!'

Gareth looked up. 'Will you two be all right down here? We shan't be very long I don't expect, not if a certain young man leads the way!'

Ginny nodded. 'Yes, we'll have a great time. We're going to try out the toboggan, aren't we, Harriet?'

'Come on, Uncle Gareth,' said David. 'The lift queue's gone now.'

'We're off, see you later.' And Gareth and David swooped across to the lift station.

Ginny stuck their skis into the ground and, taking Harriet's hand, said, 'Come on then, let's have a go.'

They stumped a little way up the hill, pulling the toboggan behind them. Then, sitting astride with their feet stuck out in front of them, they hurtled down the slope to the meeting place once more, Harriet clutching Ginny's arms which were round her waist, and screaming with excitement all the way.

They had several goes before Harriet was confident enough to try alone, but once she had done so, lying on her stomach and travelling head first, there was no stopping her. Ginny sat in the watery sun on a bench nearby and watched Harriet as she went further and further up the hill, giving herself a longer ride each time. On several occasions, she crashed into a snowdrift at the bottom, but when Ginny rushed to pull her out she seemed unconcerned and set off up the hill again at once.

Gareth and David arrived at great

speed, having *schussed* from the end of the woodland trail, as Ginny had seen the man do on her first day. They swished to a halt beside Ginny, spraying her with powdery snow and laughing with the exhilaration of their descent.

'Fan-tastic!' crowed David. 'My new skis go so fast, Ginny. You'll never keep up with me now.'

'Won't I just? We'll see about that.'

'Your turn,' announced Gareth. 'He wears me out. I'll just do a little gentle sledging with Harriet.'

'That's not so gentle either.' Ginny laughed. 'Look!'

They all turned where she pointed to watch Harriet careering down the hillside, the toboggan completely out of control, and ending up head first in a snow drift. They rushed to pull her out, but she was already on her feet by the time they reached her, shaking her head like a puppy.

★   ★   ★

69

Ginny and Gareth spent the rest of the day sharing the children between them, stopping for coffees and Cokes at regular intervals, and eating enormous meals both at mid-day and in the evening. The day slipped by without a moment spare to remember Christmases past, nor to let regret steal in. It was a Christmas Day on its own with no comparisons possible, and by the time the children collapsed into exhausted slumber, Ginny was ready to flop into a chair feeling that she never wanted to move again. Gareth poured drinks for them all and then he, too, sank into a chair by the fire, heaving an enormous sigh.

'I am exhausted.' He grinned. 'I haven't stopped all day. Where do they get all their energy from? Do you know, I think the only time David wasn't actually on the move was when he was sitting at the table eating?'

'Even then he doesn't sit still.' Mrs. Chilton laughed. She felt less shattered than Gareth and Ginny, not having partaken in the physical side of the day, but she did find the children a strain for all that, and was glad they were in bed at last. A blissful silence encompassed them all.

'Are you going out this evening?' Mrs. Chilton suddenly asked. 'Ginny hasn't been out once since we got here. She's entitled to a little *après ski*, you know.'

Ginny began to protest, and Gareth said, 'Not tonight, Mother. I couldn't move again. Tomorrow perhaps, when the children are back in ski school and we haven't got to amuse them all day.' He turned to Ginny. 'You don't want to go out tonight, do you?' It was almost a plea, and she laughed.

'No, not in the least.'

'Good. We might play a gentle game of chess, if you like.'

'When I've finished my drink, that would be nice.'

In the event, Gareth poured them a second drink before setting up the chess board between them. He had heard Ginny promising to teach David

71

to play the night before when David had opened her present, so he knew she could play, but he wasn't prepared for how well!

Before long, he was struggling, and when she smiled wolfishly and said, 'Checkmate, I think you'll find,' he discovered she had beaten him in fifteen minutes flat.

He regarded her obliquely for a moment and then said, 'Revenge?'

The second game took longer. Gareth played far more carefully, considering his moves and watching for Ginny's reaction to them. She schooled her face to impassivity, giving him no clue to her thoughts, and it was a while before either of them got the upper hand. Ginny was amused at how carelessly he had played the first game. He must have thought she would be easy meat, but now he was determined not to be beaten again it took her much longer to accomplish it.

* * *

Next morning, the children were back in ski school, David proudly displaying his new skis, and Harriet only going after Gareth had promised faithfully to toboggan with her at lunch time. It was a much colder day. The leaden clouds defeated the sun's efforts to pierce them, and Harriet's ski instructor forecast snow.

'But there is no worry if it snows,' she said. 'The children will not be cold. I take them into the ski school house and we play. You can meet them there at the usual time.'

Once they had dealt with the children, Gareth said, 'Come on, or we'll freeze.' Ginny followed him down to the lift station. She hadn't known if he wanted her to ski with him, as he'd said nothing on the subject. Now it was clear he just assumed she would. She didn't really mind. The tension she'd felt between them in London had eased gradually since his arrival in Austria and, as she watched him with the children, her initial antipathy dispersed.

The children obviously loved being with him and she had to admit that she had enjoyed the previous day as much as they had; he could be very good company.

So he proved that morning. They skied fast and hard, but while waiting for lifts, and side by side on the double chair, he was cheerful and amusing. When they stopped for a coffee in the little restaurant on the highest peak, he took the trouble to draw her out, so that Ginny felt he had a genuine interest in her thoughts and ideas.

They finished their coffee and, donning ski hats and gloves once more, left the comforting warmth of the restaurant to find the clouds had closed in round the peaks. It was snowing hard and a biting wind had sprung up, piercing the padded warmth of their ski suits.

'Come on, we must get down,' said Gareth. 'Can you see the markers?'

Ginny peered into the driving snow. It was almost a white-out, and for a moment she wasn't even sure which way was down, let alone which direction to take to stay on the marked *piste*.

'There's one over there,' she said, pointing. Other skiers were emerging from the restaurant hut now, and so, joining together in a small group, they headed for the first marker. Pausing beside it, they could just make out the second, and so going steadily, almost unable to see as the snow stuck to their goggles, they skied to the next post and scanned the hill for the third one.

'You all right?' called Gareth as they reached it.

'Yes, fine. Jolly cold, and I can't see much. I'll be glad to get to the bottom.'

'Me too,' said Gareth. 'Ready?'

'Yes, I'm right behind you.'

* * *

They skied down the hill and at last emerged from the clouds into the cold grey light beneath them. Coming round from the shelter of a shoulder of hillside, an icy blast hit them as the wind swept uninterrupted across the open mountain. They were still far above the tree line so there was no protection. Suddenly the wind swirled in an eddy, catching up the falling snow and turning it into a whirl-pool of snowflakes and ice crystals. Ginny swung to a halt and turned her back on the wind, covering her nose and mouth with both hands as the spindrift smothered her. Attacking her from all sides, it drove the freezing snow in under her goggles to fill her eyes, beneath her hat to fill her ears, forcing the ice crystals down her neck and into her sleeves. She cowered against the maelstrom for the few seconds it enveloped her, and emerged as snow-encrusted as if she had fallen in a snowdrift. Quickly she cleaned her goggles and banged the loose snow from her suit. She could see the spin-drift continuing its whirling progress across the hill and there was more to come. It was no time to be standing about. Without further hesitation, she turned down the mountain, almost passing Gareth without seeing him as he waited for her on the next ridge. He called to her and she skidded up beside him.

'You look like the abominable snowman,' he remarked, proffering a scarf from his pocket to wipe her face and goggles.

'I feel like him.'

'Did you fall?'

'No. Spindrift. I just had to stop, my nose was blocked with snow and I couldn't breathe.'

Gareth looked anxious. 'Are you all right now?'

Ginny shivered, but managed a smile. 'Yes. Just cold,' she said. 'Come on.'

She had known a moment of fear while caught in the whirlpool of snow, but she was determined Gareth shouldn't know she'd been afraid. She turned on down the hill, and didn't see the respect which flashed into his dark eyes as he said, 'Good girl,' and followed her.

They skied non-stop to the bottom, and by the time they *schussed* to a stop on the nursery slopes, Ginny was very hot and panting for breath. The ice crystals which had managed to creep inside her suit had melted and she felt uncomfortably wet.

'You'd better go back and get changed,' said Gareth. 'I'll fetch the children and bring them home for lunch. Tell Mother and Elisabeth we'll be coming.'

★ ★ ★

Ginny returned to the *Haus Elisabeth* immediately and, having passed on Gareth's message, sunk gratefully into a hot bath, submerging herself completely so that the water covered her from the top of her head, and warmth began to steal back into her body. By the time Gareth got home with the children, she was warm and dry and ready to eat the enormous lunch

Elisabeth had provided.

To the disappointment of the children, Gareth put a ban on outdoor pursuits that afternoon.

'I thought we'd go swimming,' said Gareth, 'and Granny can come and watch,' he added with a twinkle. Granny had shown no inclination to emerge from the house that day and, though he didn't really blame her, he knew it would give pleasure to the children if she were there to watch their exploits in the water. Mrs. Chilton knew it, too, and so after a quiet hour beside the fire, the whole party collected collected swimming things and braved the elements once more to spend the rest of the afternoon at the local sports complex.

Ginny had taken them there several times before Gareth arrived at St. Georg, so they knew their way about, and before long the four of them joined all the other skiers who had taken the afternoon off in the huge swimming pool, while Mrs. Chilton, installed in a seat near by, drank coffee and watched them swim.

When Ginny emerged from the changing room in her blue and red striped bikini, Gareth looked at her with undisguised approval, his eyes flowing over her from head to foot.

'Gareth, don't ogle the poor girl,' scolded his mother.

Ginny was made more uncomfortable by the remark than by Gareth's appreciation, but Gareth himself was quite unrepentant. He just laughed and said, 'I was going to point out that if that creation had some white in it she'd look like a Union Jack.'

'You be careful you don't fall in,' said Ginny gently, and then, with a quick push, tipped him into the water. Not quickly enough. His hand flashed out and grabbed her wrist, pulling her with him so that they both emerged spluttering from the water a moment later to the delighted squeals of the two children. An attendant came across and called out to them in a guttural tone,

'*Bitte*! No horse-play.'

Gareth grinned at David as the man walked away.

'I wasn't being a horse,' he said in an injured tone.

David hooted with laughter and cried, 'Uncle Gareth, you are funny!'

★   ★   ★

Ginny was inclined to agree, but she had also felt the strength of his grip as he had pulled her into the pool with him. Twisting away from him under the water, she had felt the heat of his hands on her arms and shoulders as she came to the surface, and she was aware it wasn't only the sudden ducking which had left her spluttering and breathless. Despite her usual carefully prepared defences, she knew how aware of Gareth she was becoming, and she felt a quickening of her pulse and a tug of excitement. She swam across to Harriet, who was fast gaining as much confidence in the swimming pool as she

81

had on the ski slopes, and it was while she was helping Harriet practise jumping in, that Ginny saw Mary Lancer sitting on the side of the pool dangling her feet in the water.

'Hello,' she called, swimming across to her with Harriet in tow. 'Have you chickened out, too?'

'You bet.' Mary grinned. 'I came on holiday to enjoy myself and there was nothing enjoyable about the conditions this morning.'

Ginny agreed wholeheartedly. Gareth and David swam up at that moment to see how Harriet was doing and Ginny introduced Gareth to Mary.

'We skied together quite a bit last week,' Ginny explained.

'Where are you staying?' asked Gareth.

'The Eidelweiss.'

'Any good?'

'Lovely. The rooms are a bit small but the food's excellent. There's a nice bar and a night club in the cellar.'

'Sounds good,' said Gareth.

'It is, really. Why don't you both come up and join us for a drink this evening?' Mary suggested. 'It'd be fun.'

'That would be lovely,' began Ginny, 'but — '

'But nothing,' said Gareth. 'Mother'll baby-sit. She's said so already. We'll join you about nine, when we've got these two into bed.' He nodded at the children. 'All right Ginny?'

'Lovely. We'll look forward to it.' And she meant it.

* * *

The snow had stopped when Ginny and Gareth set out for the Eidelweiss later that evening. The clouds had cleared a little and, though the sky was ragged, the moon shone through fitfully. The blanket of new snow gleamed coldly on the steep roofs and window ledges. Untrodden in the gardens, it sparkled in the light from the unshuttered windows. The air was crisp and sharp and, as they walked along the narrow roads to the Eidelweiss, their breath clouded before them in soft white billows.

Gareth took Ginny's arm quite naturally as they stepped along the snowy pavements. Concealed beneath the layer of powder were hard icy ruts ready to trip the unwary, and Ginny was glad of his steadying hand.

'Tell me about these people we're going to meet,' he said.

'I don't know very much,' admitted Ginny. 'They're called John and Mary Lancer and I think they come from Stockport. I've skied with them a bit, that's all. John's good. I think Mary skis to please him.'

'Well, we can always join them for a quick drink, then move on if we want to,' said Gareth cheerfully. 'I thought we might go to one of the night clubs.'

'Mary said there was one in the Eidelweiss.'

'I know, but there are plenty of others. Ah, here we are.'

Coming in from the cold outside, the

warmth of the Hotel Eidelweiss was almost overpowering. They shed their coats immediately, leaving them in a cloakroom, and crossed the hall into the bar.

It was a snug little room with red-clothed tables and an enclosed stove in one corner. There were several groups talking and laughing but there was no sign of the Lancers. Gareth bought some drinks at the bar and carried them to the last free table, near the stove.

At that moment, a man appeared at the door of the bar and scanned the tables. When he saw Ginny he waved and came towards them.

'Here's John now,' said Ginny and Gareth turned to inspect the small bearded figure approaching them, a wide smile of welcome on his face. Ginny introduced the two men and John perched on a stool by their table.

'Where's Mary?' asked Ginny.

'She's down in the night club, keeping a table. We thought you might want to dance so we went down early. It gets awfully crowded later on, so once you've got a table, it's silly to let it go. I just popped up to see if you'd arrived.'

★　★　★

They carried their glasses down the stairs to the cellar night club where Mary greeted them effusively. A band was on a small platform plugging guitars into amplifiers and setting up a drum kit. It was going to be very noisy.

'Some nights it's a disco,' said Mary, 'but tonight the music's live.'

'Did you ski this afternoon, John?' enquired Ginny.

'I did, more fool me,' John replied laughing.

'You should have seen him when he came in,' said Mary. 'His hat was almost frozen to his head, his beard was a mass of icicles, every crease and fold and pocket of his suit was full of snow, and it melted all over the bedroom floor.'

'But did you enjoy skiing in that weather?' asked Ginny incredulously.

John smiled. 'I love skiing,' he said. 'We come for only two weeks every year and I don't intend to miss a minute of it. I ski in any weather.'

'I didn't like the spindrift much,' said Ginny. 'I got caught in a sort of whirl of it this morning.'

'No,' agreed John, 'that's not at all pleasant. I remember once . . . ' and he was off into memories of previous ski trips. Gareth joined in with an anecdote or two, but then the music started and all further conversation was impossible. John and Mary got up to dance and Gareth and Ginny joined them.

The music was loud and thumping, and the dance floor small and crowded. Couples jigged about, often separated by the crush, so when at last a slower quieter tune came round, Gareth grabbed hold of Ginny and said, 'Thank goodness for something more peaceful.' Many of the people left the little floor in search of drink, but even so there wasn't much room to move.

Gareth pulled Ginny into his arms and held her close against him. She could feel his heart beating, sense his masculinity and strength beneath the softness of his clothes.

'God's gift to women,' whispered Katie in the back of Ginny's mind, and Ginny, glancing upwards, thought, 'Well he is very attractive — far more so than I first thought.'

Catching her glance, Gareth smiled down at her and Ginny turned her face away, colour flooding her face. His smile, directed exclusively at her, made her suddenly shaky and unsure of herself. With her heart beating double time, held firmly in his arms, Ginny surrendered to the mood of the moment.

They finished the dance without a word passing between them, then, as the throbbing beat of a rock number took the place of the love song, Gareth pressed his lips to her ear and said, 'Can we go now?'

Not trusting her voice, Ginny nodded and Gareth led her back to the table where John and Mary were sitting.

'A bit noisy,' he shouted above the din.

'We were thinking just the same,' bellowed John. 'If you'll excuse me, I'm going to go up to bed. I'm going to ski over to Gruneberg tomorrow with one of the instructors and another couple. It'll be a long day.'

They left their table and escaped back to the comparative quiet of the upstairs bar. They had one more drink altogether, then John and Mary bade them good night and Gareth and Ginny collected their coats and stepped out into the frosty night.

Gareth took her arm and led Ginny across the square.

She looked up at him in surprise and said, 'Aren't we going home?'

'No, not unless you want to. I thought somewhere more peaceful, where we could talk.'

They found a quiet bar in a little

alley off the main square and took their drinks to a secluded alcove near the fire. There were few others in the bar and the talk was no more than a soft murmur.

Gareth looked across at Ginny and smiled. 'This is more like it,' he said. 'Or am I getting old?'

Ginny laughed. 'I like dancing,' she said, 'but that place was impossible.'

'We'll try and find somewhere less noisy to dance tomorrow,' he said.

'Tomorrow?'

'Why not? We're entitled to our evenings off.' His eyes twinkled. 'It's hard work being an uncle!'

Ginny laughed again and said, 'Well, you do it very well.'

'You know, you're quite stunning when you laugh,' said Gareth suddenly. 'I'm glad you came instead of Katie.'

Disconcerted by his unexpected compliment, Ginny said awkwardly, 'So am I.' Inwardly she thought, 'What on earth am I doing? Pull yourself together, girl. Don't fall for his charm.

Male chauvinist, remember?' But he hadn't been behaving particularly like one. In fact, the more she learned of his character, the more she liked him. It was all very disconcerting.

★ ★ ★

But Gareth said nothing else to disconcert her. Instead he began to talk about the children again, to tell her of the arrangements he had made for their welfare. When he mentioned that they were both going to boarding school, Ginny, remembering the reaction she'd had from Mrs. Chilton when she'd passed comment, said nothing. But her heart ached for Harriet being sent away to school so young.

'What do you think?' asked Gareth suddenly. 'Will they be all right?'

'I'm sure you've done the best you can in the circumstances,' replied Ginny carefully.

Gareth grinned. 'Come on,' he said. 'Tell me what you really think.'

'All right. An honest opinion: I think David will be fine. He's older and more resilient than Harriet. He'll probably enjoy the rough and tumble of boarding school. But Harriet's different and I think she's far too young to be away from home.'

'But home isn't home as she knew it. They'll come to me during the holidays and I'll have a housekeeper or au pair or something to look after them, but it wouldn't really be practicable during the term.'

'You may find Harriet has difficulties adjusting at first.'

'I know. But I've done all I can to smooth the path for her. I've found a school which takes boys and girls as boarders, so she'll have David there with her. I know it won't be easy, but I'll watch her carefully.'

*　*　*

When they reached *Haus Elisabeth*, there were lights on in the hall and on the landing but the rest of the house was in darkness.

Gareth closed the door quietly behind them and, taking Ginny's hand, led her into the living-room. The embers of the fire glowed in the grate.

'Will you have a night cap?' he asked, switching on a table lamp and crossing to the sideboard.

'No, thank you. I think I've had enough to drink.'

In fact, Ginny hadn't had a great deal of alcohol, but she was wondering if it had gone to her head. She felt a little breathless and shaky, and had been profoundly aware of Gareth's proximity on their way home.

Now she felt the need to get away on her own, to allow herself time to consider. She had not been so physically aware of a man for a long time, not since . . . a face flickered into her mind, the face of a man now happily married elsewhere. Roger. As always, she closed her mind to his image, but this time perhaps he was a little less distinct. Casual affairs had never appealed to Ginny; she needed the commitment of a deeper relationship, yet she was afraid of being hurt. She had avoided anything approaching involvement since the days of Roger, and now feeling emotion stir within her, she needed to turn away and search her heart.

Trembling on the brink once more, she made to draw back. She was too late. When she refused the drink, Gareth turned back from the sideboard and before she could speak to say good night — or anything else for that matter — he had taken her hand and pulled her gently to him, burying his face in her hair.

For a moment she stood quiescent in his arms, though her mind was in a turmoil, then, as his lips began to explore her neck and face, she found herself responding. She raised a willing mouth to his, and abandoned herself to the ecstasy of his kisses.

When at last he raised his head, he

looked down at her and, with the faintest shake of his head, he said softly, 'Ginny, you're quite something.'

* * *

Suddenly shy at having revealed too much of herself, Ginny lowered her eyes and tried to pull free, but Gareth's arms were still about her and at her movement he swung her off her feet and carried her across to the hearth rug. There he set her down and, sitting in front of the fire, he pulled her down beside him.

Very gently he kissed her again and then said, 'Don't move, you hear?'

He threw a log on the fire and poked the embers to blaze up round it, then he crossed the room, closed and locked the door and switched out the light. The firelight danced on the ceiling and tossed shadows on the walls, and in the warm glow Ginny curled up on the hearth rug like a contented kitten.

Gareth returned to her and, slipping

down on to the rug beside her pulled her against him and began to smooth her tangled hair. Ginny put up a hand to touch his face, and he took it and placed a kiss in its palm.

'You're beautiful,' he breathed, and began to kiss her again, his lips becoming more and more demanding as he felt the response in her.

Eventually, they drew apart, and Gareth felt her trembling in his arms and held her more closely, murmuring endearments as she leaned against him, blissfully content to be there.

As the fire died away, they talked and laughed and kissed, feeling totally at one with each other. It was as if they had been close friends for years. As the warm intimacy enveloped them, Ginny allowed herself to believe that Gareth loved her. It was a wonderful feeling, one that nothing could ever destroy.

Then, the fire long gone out, like guilty children they stole through the sleeping house, hand in hand, and parted on the landing. Gareth kissed her gently.

'Sweet dreams, my sweet,' he whispered.

Ginny returned his kiss and then, breaking away said softly, 'Good night, Gareth.' And at last, still shaken by the speed of events and the power of her response, she sought the silent refuge of her room.

3

Ginny woke next morning and lay for a moment cocooned in happiness. She let her mind range back over the previous evening with Gareth, wandering through the memory, reliving the incidents leading up to their moments of closeness in the firelit room. At the recollection she felt an inward glow.

Suddenly Ginny couldn't wait to see him. She jumped out of bed and washed and dressed quickly so that she could go down for breakfast and see him across the table.

'You're like a schoolgirl.' She laughed at herself as she paused to spray on some of the perfume he had given her, and with a heart lighter than it had been for months, she stepped downstairs to breakfast.

Mrs. Chilton and the children were already at the table and as Ginny walked in, Elisabeth brought fresh coffee.

'Sorry I'm late down,' said Ginny. 'The children didn't come in this morning and I've only just woken up.'

Mrs. Chilton smiled. 'I managed to restrain them from disturbing you or Gareth,' she said. 'I thought you'd both earned a lie-in. Gareth hasn't surfaced yet. Did you have a late night?'

'Fairly,' admitted Ginny. 'We met some friends and went to a night club.'

Elisabeth was leaving the room and Mrs. Chilton called to her, 'My son isn't awake yet. Could you keep some breakfast for him, please?'

Elisabeth paused with a look of surprise. 'Your son has eaten breakfast.'

'He's had his breakfast? Well, where is he now? I wonder.'

'There was a telephone call and he left the house. He has not told you this?'

'No,' said Mrs. Chilton, puzzled. 'Did he say where he'd gone?'

'He say he must go out and there will be a person more for this evening meal.'

'Curiouser and curiouser,' remarked Mrs. Chilton. 'He didn't say anything to you, Ginny?'

Ginny shook her head. 'No, nothing.'

The day passed agonisingly slowly for Ginny. She saw the children into ski school and then skied on her own until lunchtime. Mrs. Chilton joined them in the Adler bar for a drink and a snack, and then it was back to the slopes to ski with David while Mrs. Chilton watched Harriet on her toboggan. Following afternoon ski school, they went swimming and then at last it was time to get ready for the evening.

Ginny felt a delicious anticipation as she changed into her *après ski* clothes. It took her some time to decide what to wear, but as Gareth had said they would find somewhere to dance she settled on her black velvet trousers topped with a white lace blouse. She surveyed herself in the mirror and then went downstairs. She felt good, and her inward happiness glowed in her eyes.

The living-room door was ajar as she

came down, and she heard Gareth's voice. She felt a thrill run through her and, pausing only to catch her breath, she pushed the door wider and went in.

Gareth was standing with his back to the fire and for a moment he was all Ginny saw. 'Gareth,' she cried, 'you're back.'

There was a fractional silence as the children ceased telling their uncle of the day's exploits and then Gareth spoke, his voice strangely tight and curt.

'There you are! We were beginning to wonder what was keeping you.'

'I'm sorry — I — ' began Ginny, surprised at his tone.

'Ginny, my dear,' interrupted Mrs. Chilton softly, 'I don't think you know Angela, a friend of Gareth's. She flew out today from London to join us. Gareth's just fetched her from the airport. That was the mysterious telephone call this morning.'

Ginny's smile froze and then gradually faded as she turned and saw Angela reclining in an armchair.

'Angela, this is Ginny who's come with us to help with the children.'

★　★　★

Ginny's mouth was dry. She recognised Angela immediately for what she was — Gareth's girl friend — but she managed to say, 'How do you do?' and extend her hand.

Angela made no move to get up or to take the proffered hand, but drawled casually, 'Hello there. What a lovely job to have, taking children on a skiing holiday.' She spoke easily but it was apparent to Ginny that the eyes sheltering behind fluttering lashes were agate-hard, and had quickly assimilated the importance of the clothes she wore. Angela recognised Ginny as a potential rival for Gareth's attention and was determined to establish supremacy from the start. Her sweet smile remained fixed as she turned to Mrs. Chilton and said, 'Gareth suggested we have a quiet drink out somewhere this evening. You will come with us, won't you? It would be a pity not to take advantage of having a baby-sitter on hand.' She turned her attention to Gareth who was still standing by the fire, and said, 'I'm sure you know somewhere nice to take your mother for a drink, don't you, darling?'

'Oh, I'm sure you don't want me — ' began Mrs. Chilton, but to Ginny's surprise Gareth added his weight to Angela's suggestion. 'Why not, Mother? It'll do you good. You haven't been out in the evening since you arrived.'

Mrs. Chilton looked pleased. 'Well, if you're sure, perhaps I'll join you for a little while. You hadn't arranged to go out this evening with your friends, had you, Ginny?'

Ginny, scarcely daring to trust her voice, said no, and keeping her eyes studiously away from both Gareth and Angela, offered to fulfil her promise to David and teach him to play chess after supper.

'Can I play?' demanded Harriet. 'Will

you teach me, too?'

'You can watch for a little while before you go to bed,' promised Ginny, and Harriet beamed. She liked to be involved in everything David did.

★   ★   ★

Harriet left Ginny's side and confronted Gareth. 'Will you be skiing with us tomorrow?' she asked. 'We missed you today.'

'Well, we'll have to see about that,' said Gareth. 'Some of the time I expect, yes.'

'Don't forget it's Uncle Gareth's holiday, too,' said Angela sweetly. 'He must have some time to himself.'

'He had some today,' pointed out Harriet. 'He promised — '

'I promise you won't get left out, Harri, all right? Angela can ski with us as well, can't she?'

'And Ginny,' said Harriet with satisfaction at having extracted a promise from her uncle.

'And Ginny, too, of course, if she wants to. But you must remember Ginny is entitled to some free time and may prefer to ski with the friends she has made in the village.'

Supper wasn't am easy meal. The children kept up a steady prattle, for which Ginny was grateful as it covered her own lack of conversation and appetite. When it was over at last, David demanded his chess lesson, and the Chiltons and Angela put on their coats and wandered into the village.

While the children were with her, Ginny managed to keep her voice light and cheerful. When it was Harriet's bedtime, Ginny went upstairs with the little girl to tuck her in.

As she sat on the bed, Harriet said suddenly, 'Did you know I'm going to boarding school when we go home?'

'Yes, Granny told me. Isn't that exciting?'

'Did you go to boarding school?'

'No, I didn't,' replied Ginny, 'but I often wished I could. You're lucky.'

'What will it be like, do you think?' Harriet's anxiety was apparent, and Ginny took her hand reassuringly.

'I don't know exactly, because they're all different, but I expect you'll sleep in a room with other girls of about your age. That should be fun. You'll never be short of people to play with, will you?'

'No.' Harriet was unconvinced. 'Will you write to me when I'm there, and come and see me?' she asked quietly.

Ginny hugged her. 'Of course I will. I'd love to see your school. And you must write to me and tell me all the exciting things you're doing.'

Harriet nodded sleepily and Ginny bent over and kissed her good night. 'Sleep well, Harriet. We'll have lots of fun tomorrow.'

★   ★   ★

Half-an-hour later David went to bed and Ginny found herself alone at last. She sank into one of the big armchairs by the fire and threw another log into the grate. Her action brought Gareth's similar action the night before sharply to mind and Ginny allowed herself to give vent to the anger which had been pent up inside her all evening — for it was anger more than misery that assailed her. And because she had been so readily captivated by Gareth's easy charm, the anger was directed more at herself than at him. 'Fool, fool,' she castigated herself. 'Why let a man like that destroy at one blow all the careful defences you've built up?'

She was angry, but the misery was there too. All the glowing happiness which had carried her through the day had drained away to leave her empty and sad. Loneliness flooded round her, and to combat it she closed her eyes and imagined herself at home in Somerset. This exercise only made her feel worse and so she tried to empty her mind and think of nothing. Exhaustion overtook her and, curled up in the deep armchair before the flickering fire, Ginny dozed fitfully, her mind still troubled.

Elisabeth, assuming Ginny had retired to bed, reached round the door and switched off the light. Not noticing Ginny asleep in the chair, she left her there in the dying light of the fire.

Mrs. Chilton returned to the *Haus Elisabeth* well before her son and Angela, and she, too, assumed Ginny was in bed. Without entering the living-room, already in darkness, she crept up the stairs to her own room, careful not to disturb the sleeping household.

Angela and Gareth were not so considerate, and allowed the front door to bang as they came home some time later. As on the previous night, the only lights burning were those in the hall and on the landing, and they were unaware of Ginny's presence in the darkness of the living-room.

The bang of the front door had awakened her and she was confused for a moment as to where she was; then she heard Angela's giggle in the hall and Gareth saying in a low voice, 'Quiet, Angie or Mother will hear us.'

'Ooh, quiet, quiet. We mustn't upset Mummy, must we? Naughty, naughty.' Angela giggled again. It was clear she had been drinking. 'What about another little drink?' she suggested.

★ ★ ★

Ginny froze, rigid in the chair. She must make her presence known, she must cough or something, anything to let them know she was there. But she was unable to move — she should have spoken at once, put the light on, anything, but now it was too late. Suppose they come in here, she thought. He wouldn't. Not after last night. What if he did? He'd know she'd overheard everything.

Feign sleep. That was the answer. She closed her eyes tightly ready to awaken sleepily if they entered the room. She had closed her eyes but she couldn't close her ears and, though the couple in the hall didn't come into the living-room they didn't go up the stairs either.

'You should have seen your au pair's face as she came bounding into the room this evening, like a dog welcoming its master. Still, I suppose you had to amuse yourself somehow while I was away,' Angela said.

'Really,' said Gareth in surprise. 'What a thing to say!' Then he laughed too and added, 'You shouldn't talk like that about her. She's a nice girl actually.'

Ginny, sitting in the darkness only feet away from them, felt herself going hot and cold with mortification. Her anger once directed against herself for succumbing to Gareth's charm was now directed at him, white hot. But even as she moved to declare her presence she knew with certainty that she would be the loser, her dignity and self-respect already in tatters would be destroyed beyond repair if she allowed Gareth to know she had overheard this conversation.

'You should have flown out with me as I first suggested,' Gareth went on.

'Look,' said Angela. 'After you, I'm the most selfish person I know, but even I couldn't leave my mother on her own over Christmas, could I? I told you when I'd be arriving — you didn't have long on your own.'

'Come on, Angie. Let's drop it.' Gareth's voice was husky. 'Let's have our drinks upstairs.'

Ginny gave them plenty of time before going up to her own room. Closing her door behind her, she gave vent to her tears of rage and humiliation. When at last those tears were spent she lay in the darkness, sick at heart. The conversation she had heard still echoed in her ears, and dawn was creeping over the mountains, filling the room with eerie grey light, before sleep finally overtook her and gave her a few hours' release.

★ ★ ★

How different was Ginny's waking the next morning from the blissful content

111

which had enfolded her the previous day. Gone was the warm expansive happiness which had filled her all through yesterday. She was left with a chill emptiness far worse than the bearable neutrality of emotion she had lived with before Gareth had kissed her.

She stared desolately out of the unshuttered window at a sky as leaden and grey as her own mind. Dispassionately she considered the situation. She could forgive Gareth for leading her on, even though he knew Angela was coming. But she could never forgive him for discussing her with Angela in the way he had.

Even more, though she didn't acknowledge the fact, she hated Angela for her snide comments and her contemptuous laughter, and it was thoughts of her derisive smile to be faced across the breakfast table this morning and every morning till after New Year that determined Ginny's course of action. Her immediate thought had been to leave for England, but this thought was dismissed almost before it was formed; she couldn't just walk out on Mrs. Chilton and the children with no explanation — and there was certainly no explanation she was prepared to give. Much as she ached to escape somewhere, to be alone to rebuild her broken defences, she knew she must stay.

No one knew she had overheard the conversation in the hall last night and she would make sure no one ever did. No matter how much she hurt inside she was determined that nobody should have the satisfaction of knowing it. She must carry on as she had during the first week of their stay and as far as possible ignore Gareth and Angela, though to do so totally might cause comment.

There was less than a week until New Year when Gareth was going home. Presumably Angela would go with him, and Ginny could relax again for the last few days before she returned to London.

Ginny blamed herself for allowing Gareth to entice her from the safety of her self-reserve, but her pride resolved that he should never know it.

With this resolution strong, she got up and went down to breakfast as usual with only the paleness of her face to show she was not herself. Angela greeted her with a self-satisfied smile and asked if she had slept well. Ginny answered politely but distantly, and gave her attention to the children. When Gareth joined them all at the table a moment later, Ginny responded coolly to his good morning and turned back to David, who was considering his chances in the races in two days' time.

★   ★   ★

The next few days passed far more easily than Ginny imagined they might. She had almost sole charge of the children outside the house, as Angela demanded Gareth's complete attention.

She was free to ski herself during ski school, and several times joined up with John and Mary Lancer for an hour or so. John, particularly, skied well and kept the pace hard and fast, so that by the end of the day Ginny slept well through physical exhaustion rather than peace of mind. She never skied with Gareth and Angela — she was never invited to do so — but occasionally, at demands from the children, Gareth joined them for a swim. The children didn't care if Angela came too or not — neither of them liked her — but she was usually there as well, as if afraid to leave Gareth alone with 'the au pair'.

Ginny watched her one day, lowering herself gingerly into the water. Angela was wearing a tiny bikini which revealed all her attributes to anyone who cared to look; her face was carefully made up and her auburn hair brushed into soft waves to frame her face. Once in the water she swam a sedate breast stroke up and down the pool, her head held well clear of the water, ignoring the happy splashing of Gareth and the children.

It was ridiculous, but somehow Ginny wouldn't have been surprised if Angela's hair had remained unaffected by the water, staying dry and immaculate throughout her swim. Ginny grinned at her own stupid thought and dived in to join the children. The waves she caused splashed into Angela's face and made the girl gasp with annoyance.

'That was pretty juvenile,' she snapped as Ginny surfaced again.

'What was?' asked Ginny unaware of what she had done. Angela glowered at her, treading water to wipe her eyes. She glanced angrily at the black smears on her hand. Her mascara, bought as waterproof, had not proved to be swimming pool proof, and had smudged.

'Gareth,' she called in an imperious tone, 'it's time to get out.'

Gareth swam over. 'You get out if you like,' he said. 'I'll just give the kids another five minutes.'

'I'd have thought they'd had long

enough,' she snapped and, seeing Gareth was not going to change his mind, she said, 'I'll see you in the foyer.'

★   ★   ★

She swam smoothly to the steps and Gareth watched appreciatively as she climbed out, her body gleaming as the water streamed off her.

David swam over, followed by Harriet, doing a furious dog-paddle.

'Have we got to get out?' he asked.

'Not for a minute or two,' replied his uncle. 'Angie has decided to go on ahead.'

'Oh good,' remarked Harriet with the frankness of her age. 'It's much more fun when she's not here. You're different.'

Ginny smiled to herself at Harriet's candid words and wondered whether Gareth would be angry at it, but he grinned his old grin and said lightly, 'I expect I am. Come on, race you to the other end.'

The conversation was closed in a flurry of water as all four of them swam the length of the pool. But later in the evening it came to Ginny's mind again when Gareth and Angela had gone out and she was sitting in front of the fire with Mrs. Chilton. An easiness had grown between them over the fortnight and now the old lady confided her dislike of Angela to Ginny.

'Do you think there's anything serious between them?' she asked anxiously.

Ginny was embarrassed by the directness of the question and said awkwardly, 'I really don't know, Mrs. Chilton. I don't know either of them well enough . . . '

'I do hope not,' Mrs. Chilton went on, almost more to herself than to Ginny. 'He's not the same when he's with her.'

'Never mind,' soothed Ginny. 'She's going home after New Year.'

'But so is Gareth,' pointed out his mother, 'and the children will miss him.'

'Well, at least tomorrow he's promised to watch them race,' said Ginny, trying to turn the conversation. 'David's determined to get a gold medal.'

Mrs. Chilton was diverted. 'Will he, do you think?'

Ginny laughed. 'If he doesn't it won't be for the want of trying.'

'Is he the best in his class?'

'I don't know,' admitted Ginny, 'but he doesn't have to be the best to win a gold. I understand that one of the instructors skis the course, and they add a certain amount on to his time. For instance, if your time is within twenty seconds of his you get a gold, thirty seconds a silver, and forty seconds a bronze. I don't know the exact timings, but it's something like that.'

'But what about Harriet? Surely she can't do that?'

'There's a beginners' course further round the hill. The same rules apply, but it's much easier and the time allowances are far greater. I imagine she only has to finish to win her medal.'

The day of the ski race dawned bright
and clear. The air was very cold, but
once the sun had struggled up over the
mountain crests there was an illusory
warmth to encourage both participants
and spectators out on to the hill.

David was so excited he could hardly
eat any breakfast — and only forced
down what he did eat after Ginny had
pointed out he would need all the
strength he had for racing.

The races were due to begin at
eleven, when the sun might have
softened the crust of ice on the top of
the snow, but well before that the whole
party sallied forth from *Haus Elisabeth*,
so that Gareth and David could do a
few warm up runs before David had to
collect his number and wait his turn
to race. Similarly, Ginny took Harriet
down the beginners' slopes once or
twice to give her a chance to find her
feet.

'You really have got on very well in

these two weeks,' Ginny told her as they waited for the little drag lift to take them up once more. 'It doesn't matter how you do in the race, we shall all be very proud of you; but if you just look for the gates and remember they go red, blue, red, blue, I don't think you'll have any problems.'

Harriet's race was first and David, Mrs. Chilton and Angela all waited at the finishing line, while Ginny and Gareth took up positions along the course to call out encouragement and to take photographs. Harriet was wearing number nine and, when it was her turn to go, Gareth snapped her coming out of the starting gate, a look of intense concentration on her face as she negotiated the first turn and went through the first gate.

'Hup! Hup! Hup!' called the spectators encouragingly, as Harriet turned through the last gate and *schussed* down to the finishing barrier.

Gareth, having kept well clear of the marked course was there before her and took another photograph of the triumphant Harriet, number nine, hurtling past the finishing post to the cheers of her family.

* * *

A Marshal removed her number and told her to be in the Eidelweiss bar to hear the results at six-thirty that evening. Then it was David's turn. His number was thirty-nine and he posed, ski sticks aloft, for Gareth to photograph before he began his run.

Several times he only just managed to turn himself in between the flags marking the obligatory gates and once, having entirely forgotten Ginny's advice that it was better to finish than to fall, completely lost his balance and travelled several yards almost sitting on his skis. But his speed didn't diminish, and somehow he managed to regain his feet before it was too late to turn through the next gate. In this way, he completed the course without the elegance of his sister but at several times the speed!

Six-thirty saw them all in a corner of the Eidelweiss bar, crushed in with all the other competitors and their friends to hear the results announced.

First they dealt with the beginners' race and, to her delight, Harriet found she had won a silver medal.

There was some time to wait before David's result was known, and he became more and more fidgety as the list of Gold medalists went on. Then at last he heard it.

'David Croyd. Great Britain. Gold medal.' With a crow of delight he pushed his way forward to receive his prize, and Gareth remarked in an undertone, 'Thank goodness for that — there'd have been heck to pay if Harriet had done better than he had.'

★ ★ ★

The next morning, New Year's Eve, was entirely different from the day before.

There was no sun and no blue sky. Heavy grey clouds shrouded the mountains and a dank mist crept between the houses in the village.

'Do you think you should ski in this weather?' asked Mrs. Chilton anxiously as she saw the children were dressed for skiing as usual.

Gareth glanced out of the window. 'They can if the ski school is operating,' he said, 'but not otherwise.'

David objected at once. 'I don't want to go back to ski school,' he complained. 'I can ski now. I'm a good skier. I want to come with you.'

'Not today, David,' said Gareth firmly. 'I'll take you tomorrow — there aren't any lessons then anyway, but today you must go into ski school.'

'It's not fair,' grumbled David. 'You always go with her.'

He glowered at Angela who tried her brightest smile and said sweetly, 'That's not quite true, David. Only yesterday your uncle gave up his skiing just to watch you race.'

'I didn't ask him to,' growled David, untruthfully.

'I watched because I wanted to,' said Gareth firmly, 'and I'll ski with you tomorrow. If you want to ski today, it'll be with the ski school.' The look on his face silenced David's protests, but he continued to mutter under his breath until his grandmother asked him to be quiet or leave the table.

Despite the uninviting weather, ski school was in operation when Ginny delivered the children to the meeting place. When they had arranged where to meet for lunch, Harriet went to her class cheerfully enough, and David stumped across to join his instructor with a thoroughly bad grace.

Ginny watched him to be sure he met up with his group; she was afraid in his present mood he might well defy his uncle's instructions and go off on his own. He didn't, however, and Ginny sighed with relief as she watched his class ski across to the chairlift, David safely amongst them.

'Hello, Ginny. On your own?' She turned to find John Lancer at her elbow, and smiled at him.

'Yes. I've just seen the children into their classes.'

'I'm alone, too. Mary doesn't fancy this weather, but we've only got today and tomorrow, so I'm out to make the most of them. Fancy some company on the hill?'

Ginny did, and together they rode the chairs up to the plateau above.

★ ★ ★

They skied almost non-stop all morning. The air was raw and cold, but the visibility was a little better than Ginny had expected. The light was flat, making the judgment of slope difficult, but the mist and cloud weren't as thick as she had imagined.

John kept up a punishing pace and Ginny, concentrating on keeping up, had no time to feel cold or uncomfortable. The only rests they had were riding the lifts, but then the chill did creep into their bodies and they were glad to be off and away down the hill again to keep the blood circulating.

When at last they returned to the meeting place to collect the children for lunch, Ginny felt both tired and exhilarated. John went back to the hotel to find Mary and try to get her to join him for the afternoon, and Ginny took the children to meet Mrs. Chilton in the Adler bar.

David's mood seemed to have cleared. He was his usual cheerful confident self, full of the morning's exploits.

'Fritz wouldn't let us do the black run from the top,' he said, obviously a little disappointed. 'He said some of us could do it all right, but the poor light would make it too difficult for the rest of the class.'

Ginny walked with them back to the meeting place and, as there was no sign of John Lancer when the classes had moved off, she decided to ski a little on her own and perhaps stop for a coffee at the restaurant at the top. She took the first chairlift and then, using the draglifts on the plateau above, had several short runs before crossing over to the double chair and beginning the long ascent to the highest point.

She shared the chair with a middle-aged German who, on establishing that Ginny came from England, chatted to her throughout the ride in impeccable English. About halfway up, huge flakes of snow began to drift down from the heavy grey sky. They twirled aimlessly in their descent, often alighting on the chairs and their occupants.

The German glanced up at the louring sky and said, 'There will be a great deal of snow, I think. The light is getting worse.'

Ginny agreed and peered anxiously through the falling flakes.

'We should not stay for long on the mountain top,' said the German. 'We can ski down together, if you like to. It is better not to be alone if such bad weather is coming. My name is Hans.'

Ginny introduced herself and said she would be very pleased to ski with him. She didn't like the look of the closing sky at all.

When they reached the end of the lift, they had quite a covering of snow on their skis and both of them were very cold. Ginny had been looking forward to a cup of coffee to warm her up before skiing back down to the village, but at her new friend's insistence they didn't take the time, and they set off at once.

The first few hundred yards Hans took very steadily, pausing occasionally to let Ginny catch her breath, but once he was certain she could ski well enough to keep up, he set a spanking pace and they hissed downward, the snow whirling in their faces, the light becoming increasingly flat. Once or twice they stopped to clear the snow from their goggles, but otherwise they skied straight down into the valley and finally came to rest, exhilarated and breathless, outside the café at the foot of the single chairlift.

Laughing together, they removed their skis and stumped gratefully inside for their coffee.

Ginny kept an eye out, watching for the children, and when she saw the ski classes coming down she thanked Hans for his company and the coffee, and braved the cold once more to meet them.

* * *

After the snug warmth of the café, the outside air was bitter and Ginny gasped as it penetrated her lungs. She picked up her skis and hurried over to where Harriet's class was removing its skis.

'I'm glad you're here, Ginny,' Harriet cried. 'We've finished early because it's so cold and horrid. I'm frozen.'

'Well, we'll just collect David,' said Ginny, 'and then I'll treat you both to a hot chocolate before we go home.'

'Ooh, great,' said Harriet, clapping her hands and stamping her feet in an effort to keep warm.

4

All the classes were finishing early and, though the lifts were still running, clunking above them as they waited, few skiers were keen enough to go back up the mountain with the warm glow of the cafés and bars to entice them in.

It was several minutes before David's class arrived. Ginny was just about to send Harriet into the café to wait there, when through the murk Ginny heard Fritz's familiar yodel and saw him cruising down the final slope with a trail of boys behind him.

'Here he comes,' cried Ginny, and they crossed to meet the class as it skidded to a halt. Ginny looked at the faces of the children, some glowing, some pinched with cold, but with a sudden lurch she realised there was no sign of David.

'Harriet,' she said sharply. 'Harriet,

where's David?'

'Don't know,' said Harriet. 'I can't see him.'

A creeping fear began to fill Ginny and she clutched hold of Fritz as he turned towards the village. 'Fritz, where's David?'

'I'm sorry?' Fritz raised his eyebrows enquiringly.

'David. David Croyd. He's in your class.'

'Ah, David,' cried Fritz. 'This afternoon he is not in class.'

'What!' cried Ginny. 'Where is he?'

Fritz shrugged. 'He come and say this afternoon he meet friends at the top station. He ski with them, I think.'

'Did he go up to the very top?'

'Maybe. I think yes, because he liked the black route.'

'Could David manage it?'

'He falls a little, but he can do. If the friends are there it is good.'

★ ★ ★

Ginny thanked him and turned back to Harriet, her brain quickly considering the possibilities. It was quite possible David had found Gareth and Angela and was safely with them. He might even be at home already. If she went home to look and found he wasn't there, the lifts might have stopped running and she would be unable to go back up to the top. She could, of course, alert the emergency services and start a full scale search, but if she did that and he turned out to be in a bar with Gareth somewhere or toasting his toes at the *Haus Elisabeth*, she would have caused a great commotion for nothing.

It would be better if she went back up to the top station and skied down the black run to find him. If he wasn't there and not safely home when she got down, she would alert the mountain rescue.

The decision made, she turned to Harriet. 'Now, listen, love,' she said, 'David's gone off on his own. The run he's doing is more difficult than he thinks and so he'll take longer than he thinks. I'm a bit worried he may get caught in the dark. You walk on home, and tell Granny I've gone up to find him and we'll be home soon. If you find him at home tell them not to come looking for me or we may all miss each other in the snow. All right? I'll be back soon one way or another.'

Harriet nodded, wide-eyed.

'Good girl. Run on home to tell Granny, or Uncle Gareth if he's there, and I'll go up again before the lifts stop. Leave your skis in the rack by the café, we can always pick them up later.'

★ ★ ★

Harriet set off slowly towards the café, carrying her skis, and Ginny hurried to the lift station. Written up on a blackboard were the words 'Last ascent sixteen hundred hours'. She glanced at the clock on the lift station. It was fifteen forty-five. The chairlift took ten minutes which would give her five more minutes to cross to the double chair and take its last ride — provided, of course, that its last ascent was at the same time.

The lift attendant spoke little English and Ginny didn't waste precious minutes trying to ask him about the second chairlift. She swung herself on to the first one and was carried out over the meeting place and up into the grey gloom above. The snow was still falling steadily, making visibility very poor, but throughout her ride she kept her eyes glued to the trails below her in the hope of seeing a small lone figure on his way down. But she saw no one the right size, and her heart grew heavier.

As soon as she slid from the chair at the middle station, Ginny set off to ski across to the bottom of the double chair. It was far windier up here above the tree line without the shelter of the valley. She reached the second chairlift with two minutes to spare. The lift was still running and, with a glance at the clock, the attendant allowed her to board. As she climbed on to the slowly moving chair, she heard a clanking noise and, looking down, saw the man chaining off the entrance to the lift. No one else would follow her up the mountain today.

The journey to the top station had been a long cold one earlier in the afternoon when Ginny had had Hans for company. Now, on her own, it seemed longer and colder than ever. By the time she finally reached the top, she was thoroughly chilled, her hands and feet completely numb, and the parts of her face not covered by goggles and hat were white with cold.

★   ★   ★

She decided to look in the restaurant first, and skied across towards its welcoming lights. As she moved away from the lift station, the sound of the lift's motor died away, leaving an eerie silence behind it. When she reached the restaurant, Ginny took off her skis and went inside. A blast of warm air hit her as she opened the door and a guffaw of laughter from a group at a corner table, who were fortifying themselves with schnapps before facing the long cold ski back to the village. There was no sign of David.

Ginny crossed to the counter and spoke to the waitress there.

'Was there a boy here earlier?' She described David and the waitress shrugged.

'Many peoples,' she said. 'Franz!'

A man in shirt sleeves appeared from a room at the back, and the waitress spoke to him rapidly in German. Franz nodded and replied.

The waitress turned back to Ginny. 'A boy was here. Maybe your boy.'

'Was he alone?' asked Ginny, praying Gareth had been with him.

The woman repeated the question and Franz nodded again. 'Ja. Ja.'

'Did you see him leave? How long ago?'

They consulted together again and then the waitress said, 'Not long. Franz says maybe fifteen minutes.'

She thanked them and set her face to the cold outside once more. Two routes started from outside the restaurant, one marked with red markers indicating medium difficulty and the other with black. Ginny stood in the swirling snow and wondered. Which route should she follow? Which had David taken? Had he really tried the black in such conditions or had he enough common-sense to go for the red? If only there was someone with her, they could have taken a route each. Then she remembered the group in the café. Perhaps they could help.

⋆ ⋆ ⋆

Ginny returned to the warmth once more and, approaching the table, said, 'Excuse me, do you speak English?'

Smiling faces turned to her and one man said, '*Ja*. Little, little.'

Ginny said slowly, 'A boy, ten years,

138

has skied alone. Maybe he has difficulty, you understand?'

'*Ja. Ja.*' The man nodded, still smiling, so Ginny could only hope he really did understand what she was saying.

'Which route will you ski to the village — red or black?'

The man looked puzzled and said, '*Bitte?*' and Ginny searched her limited vocabulary for the German words.

'*Rot?* Or *Schwarz?* You?' She jabbed at him with her finger.

'Ah, *ja, ja,*' the man cried, his understanding returning, and after a quick word with his companions said, 'We ski *rot.*'

'Will you look for the boy when you ski down? I will ski the black route. *Schwarz,*' she added, tapping herself on the chest.

The man nodded vigorously and, tapping himself on the chest said, '*Rot. Rot.*'

'Thank you, thank you very much. *Danke.*'

Ginny turned once more to the door, only to be halted by a familiar voice.

'Ginny, are you up here alone?' It was John Lancer, emerging from the door marked '*Herren*'.

'Oh, John, thank goodness,' she cried, tears of relief springing to her eyes, and quickly she explained the situation.

'Right,' he said. 'I'll ski the black with you.'

They hurried out into the snow once more. The light was very poor, but darkness had not yet overtaken them. 'You follow me,' said John, 'and we'll keep stopping and calling just in case he went off the trail.'

Ginny was so relieved not to have to ski the hill on her own that she felt the tears start again in her eyes.

He turned and grinned at her reassuringly through the driving snow. 'Don't worry,' he said. 'If he's there, we'll find him.'

★ ★ ★

John led the way very slowly down the black route, pausing at each marker to call David's name. There was no reply but the sound of the rising wind. The snow was quickly covering all previous tracks so there were few signs to warn them of anyone leaving the marked route either by mistake or by falling. Ginny called, too, her voice echoing eerily in the fading light, but there was no answer.

The mountainside was bleak and empty, its snowy crests and ridges merging together in one terrifying expanse of white, without landmark or feature emerging from the swirling snow. Part of the trail was a steep mogul field, hard packed humps of snow and ice in rapid succession. It was difficult to see where one hump ended and the next began and some of the moguls were several feet high, so that, as she turned between them, Ginny often found herself sliding rapidly sideways, and had to turn again quickly to regain her balance.

She wasn't actually following John now; it was too difficult to do so on the steep narrow slope. Each made his own way to the bottom and, the first one there would wait. As she reached the last few yards, she could see John standing in the gloom watching her somewhat inexpert descent. She waved a stick in salute and then encountered a huge mogul which fell away sharply on the downhill side.

Ginny fell with it. With a frightened scream she felt her skis slide out of control and cross, tipping her unceremoniously down the hill. She slid and rolled several yards further, her skis coming off as her safety binding broke free, and she ended up in a snow drift.

'Ginny,' bellowed John as he saw her vanish into the gloom. 'Are you all right?' He turned at once, side-stepped across to her, picking up her skis which were straddled in the snow.

Ginny struggled free of the drift and said shakily, 'Yes, I'm all right.'

★ ★ ★

John reached her, carrying her skis, and hauled her to her feet. Quickly he knocked the clinging snow from her suit so that it wouldn't melt and soak through, and Ginny took off her hat and goggles to clean the snow from those. As she did so she heard something that made her stiffen. John was just saying that they must take it more slowly from here when she grabbed his arm. 'Listen,' she hissed. 'Listen.'

They both strained their ears into the silence and after what seemed like ages the sound came again.

'Help! Please help.' The cry was weak and it was hard to tell from which direction it came, but they both heard it this time.

'David!' shrieked Ginny. 'David! Where are you?'

'I'm over here,' came the feeble reply.

'Keep calling, old son,' shouted John. 'We're coming. Keep calling, we'll find you.'

Ginny hastily stepped into her skis and, cramming her hat on once more, went after John who was following the direction of David's voice.

It took only a moment to find him, though they might well have passed him unnoticed if Ginny hadn't fallen. David was lying in a hollow in the snow, one ski upside down in the snow above him and the other, still attached, underneath him and rammed so hard into the snow that he was unable to move it. He couldn't reach to release the catch of his safety bindings, and he was twisted in a painfully awkward position, entirely unable to move.

John and Ginny were beside him in a flash, and slipped off their own skis to get down to help him. John immediately released the catch on David's binding and loosed the ski, while Ginny knelt in the snow and gathered David into her arms, holding him close so that John could pull the ski away and David could get into a more comfortable position.

The boy gave a moan of pain as she moved him and said, 'My leg. My leg hurts.' He was very cold, his face deathly white under the dark blue of his ski hat. He clung to Ginny and tears poured down his cheeks.

John took immediate charge. 'Now, David, enough of that. We've got to get you down the hill as soon as we can, or you'll have more than a hurt leg to worry about. Ginny, you put one of his arms over your shoulder and I'll take the other. We've got to try and stand you up, David. Wait till I say and then we'll all try it together. All right?'

'Yes, I'll try.' David's voice was little more than a whisper.

'Good lad. Now get ready. One, two, three, heave.' They all tried to stand, the adults pulling David up between them, but it was very difficult in the deep snow of the hollow and David collapsed again, jarring his injured leg and crying out in pain.

John spoke softly to Ginny. 'We'll never get him down like this. One of us must go for help. There'll be a telephone at the middle station. We'll get them to come for him with the blood wagon.'

'You must go,' said Ginny at once and, silencing John's protests, added, 'You ski far better than I do and will take less time to get things moving. Don't argue, John. Time is of the essence. I'll wait here and try to get him warm. He's very cold, but he can't have been here that long or we'd be too late already.'

'All right, I'll go,' said John, knowing she was right, yet loath to leave her to the cold and dark. 'I'll be as quick as I can. Here, put this round him.' He stripped off his ski jacket. 'I'll be all right,' he said as Ginny started to object. 'I'll be moving to keep warm. There's a hip flask in the pocket. Perhaps a little brandy might help.'

He bent over the prone David. 'I'm going for help. I'll be as quick as I can.

You be a good boy and do just what Ginny tells you. We'll be back as soon as we can with the blood wagon.' He reached over and kissed Ginny on the cheek. 'Chin up. Brave girl,' and with that he vanished into the snow.

'What's a blood wagon?' enquired David feebly.

'You know,' answered Ginny, 'that stretcher thing on skis.'

'Oh, that,' said David, and lost interest.

'Now,' said Ginny, 'we've got to get you warm, David, and then keep us both warm. Here put this on.' She helped him struggle into John's ski jacket, which was large enough to cover David's own ski suit.

'It's the wind that's so cold,' said Ginny once he was safely into the jacket. 'Here, you have a drink of this.' She handed him the little leather-covered flask from John's pocket. 'Not too much, mind.'

David obediently took a pull at the liquid and coughed and spluttered as the brandy burned down his throat. Ginny took the flask from him and had a mouthful herself.

★ ★ ★

'Now, David,' she said briskly, 'I'm going to try and make a windbreak. While I'm doing it, swing your arms wide and shut, wide and shut, to keep your circulation going. I know you can't really move your legs much but try banging them with your hands — anything you can think of to keep warm. Good,' she said approvingly as he began to do as she'd told him. 'Keep doing that.'

Ginny then gave her attention to the wind. Quickly she picked up both her skis and David's and rammed them, tails first, into the snow side by side, so that they made a narrow wall behind the boy. Then she put the sticks in beside them and began packing the gaps with snow. She dug furiously with both hands, delving into the soft snow and packing it hard round the skis and sticks to make a more solid wall.

She eased David into its shelter and continued to burrow into the bottom of the hollow, throwing up snow on either side until she had managed to create a circular shelter to protect them from the wind; but it gave no shelter from the continually falling snow.

'Damn,' she said aloud. 'I should have made the skis into a roof.' At once she began to pull the skis free of her structure. It was no easy task, for she had packed the snow hard round them, but at last she managed it and, pulling them clear, stretched them across the walls of the little shelter. Then she climbed out and piled snow on top of them until they were almost invisible.

Satisfied at last, she filled the gaps the skis had left in the walls of her shelter and then crawled in underneath it.

'Please, God, don't let the whole thing cave in,' she begged, 'or we'll both be buried alive.' But it was a risk she

149

felt they had to take. It was appreciably warmer in the shelter and she knew neither of them would last long outside.

'Come on, David,' she said. 'Come right into the igloo and get warm.'

David had tried to keep his arms moving but it was tiring and he lacked the energy to keep going, even though he, too, realised how close they were to death. Ginny, however, had warmed up with the exertions of building the shelter, and she pulled the boy close against her, trying to warm him with the heat of her own body.

David yawned and Ginny was immediately alarmed. She had heard somewhere that if you went to sleep in the freezing cold you never woke up again.

'Now, David,' she said sharply, 'no going to sleep. Come on, we'll play a game. What shall we play?'

'I don't know.' David's weary voice said that he didn't care.

'Well, we'll play boys' names. We get three lives each and there's a pound prize.'

'I don't know that game.' David showed little more interest than before but Ginny didn't give up.

'I say a name and you have to say another, beginning with the letter at the end of the name I say. Ready?' She felt him nod. It was almost completely dark in their shelter, and that, too, seemed to make it more difficult to stay awake.

'Right. Peter. Now you have to think of a name beginning with R.'

'Richard.'

'Good — now that's a D for me. David.'

It was very simple and rather boring, but it did keep them awake. Ginny rubbed David's arms and legs and then made him sing — stupid songs, anything to keep him from dozing.

★ ★ ★

How long they were there she didn't know. All the time they were playing and singing, her ears strained for sounds of rescue. She tried to calculate

151

how long it would take John to raise the alarm and then how long it would be before the rescuers could reach them. They would have to go right to the top before they could ski down to where she and David were huddled.

Despite the continuing games and songs, her mind ranged over the day. If only she and Hans had stopped at the top for a coffee instead of hurrying on down to the restaurant at the bottom, they might have met David before he set off alone. If only she had watched him into ski school that afternoon, actually seen him move off with his class. What had been going on since Harriet had returned to the *Haus Elisabeth* without her? Gareth and Mrs. Chilton must be frantic by now. Gareth. How she wished he were here.

She kept talking to David, demanding answers. Then she remembered a bar of chocolate she had stuffed into her pocket that morning and, breaking it into pieces, she made him eat it. It was as she fed him the last piece that she heard the sounds she had been waiting for, the sounds which made her weep with relief: men's voices calling. She clambered out of the shelter to see flashes of light as they approached.

'Over here,' she called. 'Over here.' Her voice was weak and at first they didn't hear her — but she called again and suddenly they were there, John and three other men, two of them with the blood wagon between them.

It was the work of minutes to lift the injured child out of the makeshift shelter, wrap him in blankets and strap him on to the stretcher. Then, with lights blazing ahead of them once more, they set off downhill at a tremendous rate, the blood wagon skimming over the snow.

The third man and John stayed with Ginny. Weak with relief that David was now safe and suddenly overcome by the bitter cold of the night, she began to shiver; great convulsive shudders shook her body and she found her legs no longer supported her. Unable to stand, she flopped down in the snow.

John looked at her anxiously. 'Are you all right?' he said. 'Will you be able to ski down if we go one in front and one behind?'

Ginny stared up at him and a tiny section of her mind noticed he wasn't wearing his own ski jacket. Of course, David had it on.

She tried to answer his question, she tried to say, 'Yes, of course I'll be fine,' but her voice wouldn't obey her and no sound came out.

'She is too cold,' said the other man abruptly. 'Come, I take her.'

Bending down, he picked her up as easily as he had picked up David minutes earlier. Then, effortlessly, he swung her up across his shoulders and said to John, 'I will carry her to the lift. You must go before with the light.'

'Hold on, Ginny,' said John, in case she could hear him, but fairly certain she had fainted. 'It's not far from here to the middle station.'

* ★ ★ ★ *

Ginny had not, in fact, passed out, but she had no energy to answer. It was uncomfortable slung across her rescuer's shoulders, but it meant they could travel faster, and all she could think of was getting warm.

John was right and they reached the middle station very quickly. There, after a brief discussion with the other man, John said, 'You can go on down as you are or they'll put you on the lift.'

As he spoke another man appeared from the lift station carrying two large grey blankets. He lifted Ginny off her rescuer's back and, holding her firmly so that her legs didn't fold under her again, he and John swathed her in the blankets.

'Is quickest on Kurt's back,' said the man, with one look at Ginny's fatigued face, still deathly white from the cold.

Still wrapped in the blankets, the big man took Ginny on his shoulders again. She rested her face against the back of his jacket, and closed her eyes.

Then suddenly it was all over. Willing hands lifted her from Kurt's back once more and voices bubbled round her. A crowd had gathered at the bottom of the hill on hearing of the rescue. Ginny forced her eyes open again and tried to take stock of her surroundings. She saw Mary Lancer run to John and fling her arms about his neck.

She longed to cross over and tell Mary that, without John, David and she would have died up there on the cold hill, but she still seemed unable to take command of her legs. She was standing with support now, still draped in blankets, but she couldn't walk. Suddenly someone burst through the crowd and rushed over to her. Ginny saw it was Gareth, white-faced and afraid.

'Gareth, I'm so sorry,' she tried to say but her voice remained a whisper.

Gareth came to her and put his arms round her, soothing her gently, speaking as he spoke to Harriet after one of her nightmares.

'It's all right, Ginny. It's all over. You're safe, David's safe. It's all right. I've come to take you home.'

* * *

As they approached the door of the *Haus Elisabeth*, Elisabeth herself flung it wide and stood back to allow Gareth to carry Ginny inside. As he brought her into the hall, Angela emerged from the living-room and watched him.

'So,' she drawled, 'the little au pair has managed to creep back into your arms somehow, has she? What a touching sight!'

Ginny was too tired to care about Angela's spitefulness, but Gareth was not. To her surprise, Ginny felt his arms tighten round her, holding her to him almost protectively, and then she heard him speak in a tone that would have chilled her to the bone had it been directed at her.

'You sicken me, Angela. Ginny has just risked her own life out there to save

157

David's and all you can do is to make petty jibes. Now, get out of my way and let me get Ginny to her room. The doctor will be here in a minute or two.' He pushed past Angela to reach the stairs.

'Some New Year's Eve,' she shrieked after him. 'I'm leaving.'

Gareth ignored her and said to Elisabeth, 'Would you mind coming up here, Elisabeth, please. I'll need your help to get her into bed.'

Ginny was still clinging to Gareth as he carried her into her bedroom, and he had to unfasten her hands before he could lower her on to the bed. Quickly he closed the shutters and turned as Elisabeth came in.

'Will you get her out of her wet clothes, please?' he said. 'I'll go down and fill hot water bottles.'

'There are many in the bathroom,' said Elisabeth. 'Fill all in the kitchen,' and she set to work to strip Ginny's freezing body of its wet clothes and to towel her down.

Angela was waiting for Gareth in the hall, but he had little time for further conversation. He brushed past her, carrying an armful of hot water bottles, and headed for the kitchen. She followed him, trying a change of tactics.

'I know Ginny's been very brave,' she said winningly. 'She was marvellous to stay up there with David, but they're both safe now, and in good hands — David at the doctor's house, and Ginny here with the doctor calling in at any moment. Surely Elisabeth can cope now. We were supposed to be going out, remember?'

Gareth was busily filling hot water bottles and didn't reply at once.

Encouraged by his silence Angela went on, 'We could pop into the doctor's house and see how David is; your mother, too. We could tell her about Ginny and let her know where we'll be.'

'We'll be here,' said Gareth briefly. 'I'm not going anywhere else tonight. As you say, David's in good hands.

There's no need to disturb him again.'

'Oh, this is all horrid,' cried Angela petulantly, pouting at Gareth in a way which had never failed to make him kiss her before. 'I wish I'd never come.'

Collecting the filled bottles in his arms Gareth turned to face her. 'So do I, Angela.' He moved towards the door to carry the bottles upstairs only to find Angela once more barring his way.

'You've got yourself caught,' she taunted and laughed in derision. 'You, the great ladies' man, have fallen for a feeble little fool like that.'

*   *   *

Gareth looked directly in her eyes, contempt cold in his own and said, 'Possibly, but it's better than falling for a selfish witch like you!' Her hand flashed out at his words and slapped him across the mouth. 'How dare you?' she hissed.

But Gareth had nothing more to say to her and, thrusting her aside, he went upstairs. Elisabeth had completed her task and together they placed the hot water bottles round Ginny and drew the covers back over her.

'Now I make some tea, *ja*? For all. You stay here and I bring it.'

'Thank you,' said Gareth, 'that would be marvellous. Where's Harriet?'

'She has gone with Mrs. Chilton to doctor house,' replied Elisabeth. 'Mrs. Chilton not wants to leave Harriet with other lady.'

'Fine. The doctor should be here soon. I told them I'd bring Ginny home and he said he'd come over when David was comfortable.'

Elisabeth nodded. 'I bring here when he comes,' she said and left the room, quietly closing the door behind her.

Gareth turned back to the bed and found Ginny watching him. He drew up a chair and sat down beside her. 'Are you feeling warmer?' he asked gently.

Ginny nodded. 'Much,' she whispered.

'Elisabeth's gone to get some tea,' he said.

Ginny looked up at him, and saw his face still pale and anxious. She wanted to tell him how sorry she was that she hadn't seen David into ski school.

Gareth seemed to know what she was thinking, for before she could say anything, he took her hand from under the covers and, holding it tightly in his, said, 'Now I want you to know that you're in no way to blame for today's troubles. If anyone is, it's me. I should have taken him skiing. I knew he was longing to show me how much he'd improved on his new skis. I should have gone but I was too selfish and didn't want to give up my time with Angela.' He gave a bleak laugh.

'But you,' he continued softly, looking down at Ginny with gentle eyes, 'you saved his life. The rescuers said if you hadn't built that shelter, David would have died up there — and you, too, probably.' Still holding

Ginny's hand he placed it to his cheek and said, 'What a fool I've been.'

* * *

At that moment, Elisabeth brought in the tea and Gareth moved away from the bedside to allow her to help Ginny drink hers.

Before it was finished, the doorbell rang and Gareth went down to let in the doctor, who had Harriet with him.

'Your mother stays with the boy,' he announced. 'Harriet comes to you.'

Harriet did just that, burying her face against Gareth's body, clutching at him with her arms. He held her close and, looking down at her, he hoped that today's accident wouldn't be another source of nightmares for the little girl.

'How's David?' he asked over her head.

'As well as can be expected,' replied the doctor. 'His leg isn't broken but the knee is badly wrenched. No more skiing this year. He suffers from exposure, but he will be well again soon. You need not to worry for him — he sleeps in my house tonight. Tomorrow he can return here. Now, the young lady, please.'

Gareth led him upstairs and left him, with Elisabeth in attendance, to examine Ginny. Then he took Harriet into the living-room, poked the embers of the fire to a blaze, and read her a story. They were interrupted only once before the doctor came back down, and that was by Angela's departure. It was noisy and dramatic and it left them both with a feeling of relief.

The doctor gave Ginny something to make her sleep and, when she finally roused herself in the morning, she felt muzzy but warm. Elisabeth arrived with some hot chocolate and some toast, followed by Gareth who told her that on no account was she to try to get up.

'You're to stay there all day,' he said, 'and if you feel better enough you can come down for dinner. Doctor's orders,

not mine, though I thoroughly endorse
them.'

★   ★   ★

Ginny was quite happy to follow these
instructions and slept a great deal
during the day. When she was awake,
Harriet came in and told her David
was home. Mrs. Chilton sat with her for
some time after expressing her soft but
heartfelt thanks for what Ginny had
done.

Gareth didn't come back in to see
her, but when Ginny had decided she
would come down for the evening meal,
he was already in the living-room. After
they had all eaten, Mrs. Chilton went
up to see Harriet into bed, saying she
would go to bed herself, as she hadn't
slept much the night before.

'I think I'll go up, too,' said Ginny,
suddenly uncomfortably aware of
Gareth so near her, and not wanting
to be alone with him.

'Won't you have another cup of

coffee first?' he asked. She was about to shake her head when he went on, 'Please stay a moment. I want us to talk.'

Ginny looked surprised, dreading what he was going to say, and asked, 'Talk? What about?'

'Well.' Gareth was hesitant and he set down his coffee cup untouched. 'First I want you to promise to hear me out, without interrupting. Will you?'

Ginny managed a smile. 'I'll try,' she said.

For a moment silence slipped between them, broken only by the hissing of a damp log on the fire. Ginny waited while Gareth searched for words.

Then he started abruptly, 'You know Angela's gone?'

Ginny's lips tightened and she nodded.

'The night before she arrived . . . I'd forgotten she was coming. I mean, well, I knew she was coming but I'd forgotten when.' Gareth looked at Ginny's pale face. 'Being with you put her out of my mind, it's as simple as that. And when she did come — '

'And when she did come you returned things to the status quo.'

'I tried to, I'll admit that,' said Gareth, 'and I'm sorry you were hurt by it — but I was afraid. I've had lots of girl friends, Ginny, you know that, but I've never become involved, emotionally involved, I mean. I always cut and run before that. But with you it was different. It began the usual way, and then suddenly I was in way over my head, and it scared the life out of me. So, Angela was the perfect get-out.'

'And now she's gone, too. How disappointing for you.'

'But Ginny, Angela means nothing to me — I'm glad she's gone. It's you I want. You mean everything to me.' He looked across at her, his eyes dark and intense. 'I love you.'

'Those aren't words I use a lot,' remarked Ginny carefully.

'I've never used them before in my life,' said Gareth quietly. 'I didn't even admit the fact to myself until I thought you might be dead up there on the mountain. Then the simplicity of it all hit me like a sledge hammer. I couldn't live without you.'

Ginny looked across at him. Her blue eyes were indifferent as she said coolly, 'I'm afraid you're going to have to.'

Gareth stared at her. 'What? What are you saying?'

'I'm saying you're going to have to learn to live without me.'

'But I love you.' Incredulity crept into his voice. 'Ginny — '

'But I don't love you.' Ginny spoke firmly.

'Ginny, darling, I want to marry you.'

'Gareth, I'm sorry. I don't want to marry you.' Ginny got unsteadily to her feet and Gareth leapt to his — reaching out a hand to steady her, perhaps to draw her into his arms, Ginny didn't know and so avoided the hand.

'Ginny!' He barred her way for a moment and did capture her hands in his own. 'Ginny, we made a bad start. I hurt you unforgivably, I know. But don't turn me away now. Couldn't we start again? Please?'

Ginny quietly disengaged her hands and, ignoring the plea in his voice said, 'No, thank you, Gareth. I don't want to start anything with anyone, least of all you.'

It was enough. He moved aside and she stepped past him. As she reached the door she turned back and said softly, 'Good night, Gareth.'

★   ★   ★

Ginny slept well despite the despondency she felt after her conversation with Gareth. A few days earlier she might have rejoiced in the fact that she had the power to wound him — might have derived pleasure from getting a little of her own back — but now she felt faintly sorry he should suffer on her account. She wasn't a person who enjoyed inflicting pain on anyone. Even so, she wasn't prepared to let him break down her defences a second time.

She wasn't, however, put to the test, for when Ginny came down for a late breakfast, Mrs. Chilton told her Gareth had left for England.

When she saw Ginny's surprise she said, 'He always intended going home today, you know, and once he was assured of yours and David's recovery there was no need to stay.'

'No, of course not,' agreed Ginny hastily. 'It's just that I lost track of the days.'

'I'm not surprised at that, my dear,' said the old lady. 'We've all been at sixes and sevens. We're supposed to be leaving on Saturday, but I think we might go sooner if David's fit to travel. What do you think?'

Ginny thought it would be an excellent idea. Suddenly she wanted to go home, to retreat to the sanctuary of her own flat.

They travelled three days later and, as Ginny let herself into her own flat she was surrounded by a deep and healing stillness. Its quiet familiarity was a balm to her depressed spirits and she opened her heart to it.

* * *

Ginny visited her parents that weekend and found Katie and Don were there, too. They all asked about the Austrian job and Ginny gave them a carefully edited version, and then found herself immersed in Katie's wedding plans. The date was set for the Easter holidays, and Katie was entering into the arrangements with the enthusiasm with which she did everything.

For half-an-hour early on the Saturday evening, Ginny found herself alone with Don in the sitting-room. She sat watching the flames curling round the logs in the grate and listening to the slow majestic tick of the grandfather clock. The curtains were already drawn against the January night and, back in her childhood home, Ginny felt some of the tension which had been with her since her night on the mountain with David slip away.

Don looked up from the paper he had been reading and grinned across at her. 'Peaceful, isn't it?' he said.

Ginny laughed. 'Katie always was a human dynamo. You'll have to get used to that.'

'Oh, I'm used to it already,' asserted Don, 'but it is nice when she occasionally stops.' He paused for a moment and then said, 'I gather Gareth Chilton was out there with you. Nice chap, don't you think?'

'Yes, he can be charming. Katie doesn't like him, though.'

'Well, she wouldn't, would she? You can see at once that she and Gareth would strike sparks off each other all the time.'

'I suppose so,' agreed Ginny, 'but I didn't know you knew him.'

'Known him for years on and off,' said Don. 'His mother's an old friend of my mother's. Don't see him much these days. Dreadful about his sister, wasn't it?'

'It was,' agreed Ginny. 'Especially for the children.'

'Yes, what's happening about them? Gareth having to look after them?'

'Partly, but they're going to boarding school. They start next week.'

'Isn't the little one a bit young for that?'

Ginny nodded. 'I think so,' she said. 'I'm afraid she may feel very cut off and lonely. She's put my address down in a little address book someone gave her and says she's going to write to me often.'

'She obviously took to you,' said Don.

'Yes, I think she did. I think they both did.'

* * *

After her Somerset weekend, Ginny had to return to the hard grind of trying to find herself another job. It was certainly no easy task and she found herself becoming demoralised as she drew blank after blank.

Days crept by and turned into weeks, and Ginny began to feel the pinch of being unemployed. The weather was cold and bleak with long days of endless rain. It did nothing to raise Ginny's spirits and meant she had to trail her work round in the wet.

One day early in February she took the Tube to the City. An old art school friend had mentioned a small advertising agency he knew of in a little street off Ludgate Hill.

Without any real hope at all, Ginny had made an appointment to visit them and present her portfolio. It took her a little while to find the offices of the Bridgetown Agency but at last she found them on the third floor of a building which also housed a firm of accountants and a dentist's surgery. It all looked very unpromising from the outside, but with a sigh she opened the door and tramped up the three flights of stairs to the agency offices. There a pleasant surprise greeted her, when she found not the dingy offices she had expected but airy rooms, well lit by huge windows cut into the roof.

She was seen by the creative director, who introduced himself as Nigel Wootton, and her spirits fell as he glanced through her portfolio and said casually, 'What makes you think we might be interested in your work?'

His tone angered Ginny and, realising she had wasted her time coming and had nothing to lose she snapped, 'You ought to be interested enough to look at any work properly, particularly if it's good. And mine is.'

Nigel Wootton looked up at her with a raised eyebrow. 'Perhaps you're right,' he said, his tone as casual as before, 'but I can see it's good without having to study it.'

Ginny stared at him and then, as he said nothing more, she picked up her work and said, 'Then perhaps you'll consider using me freelance when you need someone. I'll leave my name at the desk.'

'Certainly,' he replied smoothly, 'and should anything to suit your style come in we'll know where to contact you.' He shook hands with her and closed his office door behind her.

★   ★   ★

Still annoyed, Ginny crossed to the desk in the outer office and left her name and address, then plodded down the stairs to find that the heavens had opened and raindrops the size of pennies were thudding on to the pavement. She waited in the doorway for a little while, but the downpour showed no signs of easing so at last she decided to make a dash for it.

As she rounded a corner, her head down against the rain, she cannoned into someone hurrying the other way.

The man with whom she had collided cried, 'Steady!' and caught her arm to stop her from falling, and then as she looked up to apologise, she found herself looking at Gareth Chilton.

'Ginny!' he said. 'It's you. Are you all right?'

Ginny found she was breathless, probably from running so fast, and had difficulty answering, but she nodded and, both shocked at the sudden appearance of the other, they stood for a moment in the teeming rain.

Then Gareth said, 'Here, we're getting soaked.' He took her arm and pulled her into the shelter of a doorway.

'What are you — ?'

'What brings you — ?'

They both began to speak at once and then stopped with a laugh.

'It's good to see you again, Ginny,' said Gareth. 'Have you got time for a coffee?'

'No, thank you, Gareth, I don't think so — ' began Ginny.

'Come on, just a quickie.'

Ginny didn't reply immediately and, taking her silence for acquiescence, he led her to a little coffee shop in the next street, seated her at a table by the window and ordered coffee and doughnuts for them both.

'How are the children and your mother?' asked Ginny.

'Fine,' said Gareth heartily. 'The kids are both back at school now, of course. David seems to have taken to it like a duck to water.'

'And Harriet?'

'Harri has taken a little longer to get used to it, I'm afraid, but it won't be long before she settles properly, I'm sure.'

5

The coffee came and Gareth said, 'What brings you to this part of London? Are you working round here?'

Ginny pulled a face. 'No, I wish I was. I've just been to try for a job, actually — ' she indicated the portfolio at her side — 'but it was no go.'

'Is that your work?' Gareth nodded at her case.

'Yes — or a sample, anyway.'

'Can I look?'

Suddenly shy, Ginny shook her head. 'No, it's nothing special.'

'Come on, let me see,' coaxed Gareth. 'I'd like to see what you do.'

Feeling that her work might be a safer subject than others he might broach, Ginny passed over her portfolio. Gareth unzipped it and slowly turned the polythene covered leaves. He glanced up with a grin. 'Looks pretty good to me,' he said. 'Why didn't they like it?'

Ginny shrugged. 'It may be the wrong style for their sort of work.'

'Where did you take it?'

'An agency just round the corner. The Bridgetown, it's called.'

'Oh, I know that place. I've an office in the same building.'

Ginny remembered then that it was a firm of accountants who occupied the second floor of the place. Gareth, she knew, was an accountant and must be with them. She was about to ask him when he suddenly looked at his watch.

'Good grief! Is that the time?' he said, jumping up. 'I've an appointment in ten minutes. I must fly.'

'Yes, of course.' Ginny gulped the last of her coffee and stood up, too.

'Lovely to see you again, Ginny,' he said when they were in the street again. 'Look after yourself.' He bent and kissed her lightly on the cheek and, with a wave, disappeared round the corner in the direction of his office.

* * *

Ginny, still clutching her portfolio, turned slowly towards the Tube station. It was still raining, but she didn't rush. It didn't seem to matter any more. The unexpected meeting with Gareth disturbed her equilibrium and she felt more low-spirited than she had for days. Idleness never sat well upon her and, without hard work to occupy her mind, she had found herself subject to fits of depression.

She spent the next day working on the bridesmaids' dresses Katie had press-ganged her into making.

Katie was with her when the phone call came. She had dropped in after school, ostensibly to see how the dresses were coming along but, in fact, because she was very worried about her sister. She had heard of Ginny's ordeal on the mountain through Don's mother, who had the story from Mrs. Chilton, and she wondered why Ginny had said nothing herself.

Confronting Ginny with this, Katie asked, 'Why didn't you tell us? You deserve a medal. *I* wouldn't have known what to do.'

'It was all over by then,' said Ginny. 'There was absolutely no point in worrying Mum and Dad with it after the event.'

'But you could have told me! I've been very worried about you, you know. You're not the same since you came home. Won't you tell me what happened out there?'

★   ★   ★

Ginny was saved from having to answer by the shrill of the telephone and, glad to avoid any further probing by Katie, she got up to answer it. When she returned to Katie, perched as usual on the window seat, Ginny was clearly shocked.

Katie jumped up. 'Ginny, what's the matter. You look dazed.'

'I feel it,' replied Ginny sinking into a chair. 'I've just been offered a job — at least as good as.'

Katie crowded with delight. 'Hey, that's marvellous! Who with?'

'An advertising agency I went to see yesterday. They'd nothing for me then, and now today they've rung up to offer me desk space, and say they've acquired a particular account which will suit my style.'

'What does desk space mean?' demanded Katie.

'Well, I pay them so much a week — '

'You pay them?'

'Let me finish. I pay them so much a week and for that I get a place to work and the use of all the office facilities. In return, if there's any freelance work to be done, I'm their first choice, but I'm not limited to their work alone. I mean, if I'm offered other freelance, I can use my desk space to work on it.'

'But Ginny that's marvellous,' said Katie again. 'When do you start?'

'Immediately, if I start at all,' said Ginny. 'I said I'd let them know tomorrow.'

'Let them know!' cried Katie. 'Is there any reason not to accept? Especially as they have a job ready and waiting for you.'

'Several reasons, actually,' replied Ginny with a faint smile, 'but it's a decision I want to make on my own, and when I've made up my mind you'll be the first to know — well, the second. I expect I'll tell them first. Now, have a look at these dresses and tell me if the neckline is as you visualised it.'

After Katie had gone, Ginny sat staring out of the window, her mind in a turmoil. What should she do? The offer Nigel Wootton had made was a very tempting one. It gave her a foot in the door and, if her work pleased him, she must be in with a chance of being taken on staff if a vacancy occurred. It was extremely lucky for her that her particular talents should be needed unexpectedly — he clearly hadn't needed them yesterday.

But there were two main drawbacks. One was that if the work fizzled out and no money came in, she was still committed to paying for her desk space, and the other was Gareth. His firm was in the same building as the Bridgetown Agency and there was every likelihood of her bumping into him fairly often, which was not a prospect she viewed with enthusiasm.

At last, still undecided, she went to bed, hoping a night's sleep would clarify her mind. It didn't, but her post plopping through her letter box next morning — two bills, one for the telephone and the other for electricity — did. Gareth or not, beggars couldn't be choosers and, apart from her three weeks in Austria, Ginny hadn't worked for nearly three months. The decision made, she reached for the phone and accepted Nigel Wootton's offer. He sounded pleased, and within the hour Ginny was on her way to the City to occupy her desk space.

★   ★   ★

Nigel Wootton had been right. What his client was looking for was exactly the sort of work Ginny was best at, and she settled down to several days' extremely hard work. The atmosphere in the office suited her very well and, with work to occupy her mind and her hands, she found her spirits rose naturally.

Each morning and evening, Ginny hurried on the stairs, always afraid the door to the accountants' office on the second floor would open and she would again be confronted by Gareth. But it never did, and gradually she began to relax about the whole affair. There were days when there was no work for her, and on those Ginny didn't go into the office.

She spent another weekend in Somerset with her parents and often saw Katie in the evenings when Don was working. Life returned to an even tenor, until the day when one of the art directors asked her to collect a book for him from the library. He scrawled the name on a piece of paper and Ginny set out to fetch it. When she reached the library she looked at the paper to give the title and author of the book and, as she did so, her heart missed a beat. She stared down at the paper incredulously, while the librarian asked her several times which book she had come for. Somehow she told him and thanked him when he handed it over, and then she was outside again in the fresh air. But the fresh air did little to calm her churning brain, and she had to sit down on a bench beside the river before she could begin to assimilate her discovery.

The scrap of paper carrying the book's name was a piece of the firm's headed note paper. Ginny had never seen one before or, if she had, not close enough to read the small print. Now she did read it and felt sick inside. On the right hand side was the agency's address, and on the left was the list of directors. At the top was the name Gareth Chilton, Managing Director. Underneath were other names including Nigel Wootton, Creative Director, but few of them meant anything to her and didn't concern her. All she knew was that Gareth was managing director of the agency and she owed her job to him.

'Now what do I do?' she said aloud, and the other occupant of her bench, an elderly man wearing a raincoat that had seen better days said, 'I don't know, my dear, but whatever you decide, don't be hasty.' With the advice given, he rose to his feet and shuffled off along the Embankment, leaving Ginny to ponder her predicament and the wisdom of his words.

★ ★ ★

In fact, she took his advice, and when she returned to the office and handed over the book she said nothing of her discovery until she was able to speak with Nigel Wootton alone.

'I've just seen our note paper,' she began and then paused.

'And?'

'And have learnt from it that Gareth Chilton is the managing director.'

'Well?'

'Did he tell you to take me on?'

'He suggested it,' said Nigel carefully. 'He said he'd seen your work and liked it.'

'I see,' said Ginny tightly.

'No, you don't,' said Nigel sharply. 'Gareth's in charge of finances, not the hiring and firing of staff. I liked your work too — no matter what he had said there'd have been nothing for you if I hadn't.'

'So you manufactured a job for me.'

'Not at all,' Nigel retorted. 'My, my, you are touchy. You told me yourself your work was good and, as I said at the time, you were right. After you'd gone the new work came in. I'd probably have called you anyway.'

'But Gareth asked you to.'

'He suggested we give you a try. I agreed because I had suitable work.'

'Why haven't I seen him in the office? He's never here.'

'Of course he is. He was here only two days ago, but you weren't in. He's a very busy man you know. He's on the board of two other companies and he takes his work very seriously.'

'I see.'

'Don't keep saying you see when you so obviously don't,' snapped Nigel, suddenly losing patience. 'You're here because I need you, not as a charity, but if you don't believe me, take it up with Gareth yourself. He'll be in after the weekend.'

★   ★   ★

Ginny finished her work and then, as there was nothing else for her, went home. It was a damp Friday evening, with the traffic throwing muddy spray over unwary pedestrians. Twists of fog oozed between the buildings and hung in clammy clouds above the streets, and for a moment Ginny thought, with a stab of nostalgia, of the clear sharp air of the mountains above St. Georg.

She had nothing particular planned for that evening and had promised herself a lazy hour in front of the television, but as things turned out the evening was anything but quiet. She had been home for less than an hour when the doorbell rang, Katie's long insistent ring, but when Ginny opened the door complaining that her sister need not wear the bell out, the words died on her lips. She saw not Katie, but the small woebegone figure of Harriet Croyd. Harriet stood on the landing, her hair clinging damply to her face and, on seeing Ginny, she promptly flung herself into Ginny's arms and burst into tears.

Ginny dismissed her surprise at finding Harriet outside, and held the little girl close, soothing her and calming her till the paroxysm of sobs abated somewhat, then she drew the child inside the flat and closed the front door.

Harriet pulled away, and through her tears said, 'I can't pay the taxi.'

'What?' Ginny was uncomprehending for a moment.

'The taxi. I came in a taxi but I haven't got any money.'

'All right,' said Ginny, pushing Harriet gently into the living-room. 'You take off your wet coat and wait in there.'

She went down and found the cab driver about to come inside looking for his fare.

'How much is it?' asked Ginny fumbling in her purse.

The man told her and she handed over the money. He thanked her and was about to turn away when Ginny said, 'Where did you pick her up?'

'The little girl? She found me in a cab rank off the Brompton Road. Said you'd pay when we got here.'

Ginny was surprised he had accepted the child's promise and said so.

'Well,' admitted the driver, 'I wouldn't have stopped for her if she'd tried to flag me down, but sitting in the rank and her out there in the pouring rain looking like a drowned rat, well, I couldn't leave her. I mean, anyone might have picked her up. I got kids of me own.'

Ginny thanked him again, and went back up to the flat.

Harriet had discarded her soaking raincoat and was sitting on the hearth rug, holding out her hands to the fire. Ginny switched on another bar, and then said, 'Now, I'll get a towel for your hair and make a cup of tea and you can tell me what you're doing here.'

When at last Harriet was dry, warm and comfortable again, Ginny gave her a mug of milky tea and sat down by the fire with her.

Harriet began her story. It was a somewhat muddled account of her journey up from school, but Ginny didn't interrupt her, hoping she would be able to make some sense of the whole thing by the end.

'And when I got to Granny's house she wasn't there. I waited and waited but she didn't come.' Harriet's lip trembled again. 'It was raining and dark and I didn't like it.'

'But I don't understand,' said Ginny. 'Wasn't Granny expecting you?'

Harriet shook her head miserably.

'You were going to surprise her?'

'Yes,' the child's reply was scarcely more than a whisper.

'But when you found she wasn't there, why didn't you go to Uncle Gareth? Why did you come to me?'

* * *

Harriet burst into tears again and Ginny, suddenly suspicious, said, 'Where's David?'

'He's at school,' sobbed Harriet.

'You've run away from school, haven't you, Harriet?'

Harriet nodded, still crying.

'And that's why you haven't gone to Uncle Gareth?'

'He'd send me back,' wailed the child.

Ginny didn't pursue the matter until Harriet had calmed down once more, then she said gently, 'Now, Harriet, tell me about it again from the beginning.'

'I hate it!' Harriet cried. 'I hate it at school. David's all right, he's got lots of friends. I haven't got any friends. I haven't got anyone to play with.'

'You must have,' said Ginny. 'There must be lots of girls your age who'd love to play with you.'

'But they go home,' wept Harriet. 'When lessons are finished, they go home. Their mummies take them home.'

Ginny's heart went out to the little girl who had no mummy to take her home and, close to tears herself, she gathered Harriet into her arms again.

Still holding her close, Ginny asked, 'How did you get up to London? Isn't your school in Kent?' She didn't recall its name or address but she did remember Gareth explaining it was further out than he'd have chosen, but that that was the price of not separating the children.

'I'd got enough money for the train,'

said Harriet, nestling against her. 'And when I got to Charing Cross, I remembered which bus to take. I wanted to go to Granny — she wouldn't let Uncle Gareth send me back — but when she wasn't there I didn't know what to do. Then I thought of you. I'd written a letter to you but I hadn't posted it yet. It was still in my bag so I showed the address to the taxi-man and asked him to bring me. I'm sorry you had to pay. I'll pay you back when I get some more pocket money.'

★   ★   ★

Ginny looked down reassuringly at the child's anxious face. 'Don't worry about that. You were lucky to find a taxi driver who'd take you.'

'It took a long time.' Harriet was looking a little more cheerful now that the whole story was out in the open. 'I waved at lots, but they just drove past.'

'Well now,' said Ginny briskly, 'are you hungry?'

'Starving!' replied Harriet. 'The food at school is horrid. Tinned tomatoes and porridge.'

'What, together?' Ginny laughed.

'No.' Harriet laughed, too, and Ginny was pleased to see it. 'But we have to eat it all.'

'Well, you sit here and keep warm while I find you something to eat. Will egg and bacon do?'

'Yes, please.' Harriet's reply was enthusiastic. 'And baked beans?' she added hopefully.

Ginny laughed. 'I'll see if I've got any. Now, I'll put the television on and you can sit and watch while I get the supper.' 'And ring your Uncle Gareth,' she thought.

Ginny was very loath to ring Gareth and tell him where Harriet was — it seemed to be betraying the child's trust somehow — but she knew she must contact him at once. The school would have reported the girl's absence to him by now and he would be frantic. She decided not to tell Harriet she was going to phone in case the little girl took it into her head to run off again once she knew Gareth was coming. Ginny closed the sitting-room door and hoped the sound of the television would drown her call made from the hall.

Even as she looked his number up in the phone book, Ginny knew a strong disinclination to telephone. Quite apart from letting Harriet down, Gareth was the last person she wanted to see.

★　★　★

She found the number in the book and dialled. It rang for some time before it was answered, and then a woman said, 'Yes?'

'Is Gareth Chilton there, please?' Ginny found her voice was shaking.

'Sorry, he doesn't live here any more.'

'Oh.' For an instant Ginny was at a loss then she said, 'Do you have an address or phone number for him by any chance?'

'Yes, he did leave one. Wait a minute, I'll find it.'

There was a rustling noise from the other end of the line and voices talking. Ginny stood in growing impatience, terrified Harriet would come out of the sitting-room for something and discover her on the phone. At last the woman came back and gave Ginny an address.

'Can't find the phone number,' she said. 'I thought it was on the same paper but it doesn't seem to be.'

Ginny thanked her and very carefully replaced the receiver so that the bell didn't chink. Now what should she do? She went into the kitchen and put some bacon under the grill, and was just searching for the baked beans when Harriet appeared.

'I've found the beans,' Ginny told her cheerfully. 'Won't be long. You go back by the fire, there's a good girl. Close the door to keep the heat in, will you, please?'

Reassured, Harriet did as she was told and Ginny risked another phone call; this time to directory enquiries. They regretted that the number was ex-directory.

'I'll have to go and find him,' thought Ginny helplessly. 'I'll have to put her to bed and go to this house and hope he's there.'

She went back to the kitchen and cooked the egg to go with the bacon and beans. If only she knew the name of Harriet's school, she could phone there, but she couldn't remember it and didn't want to ask Harriet. She was just dishing up when the phone rang. She called Harriet in to eat before answering it, and then picked up the receiver. It was Katie just ringing for a chat.

Ginny cut her short. 'Can you come over this evening?' she asked in a low voice.

'Well, I could I suppose,' said Katie. 'Why, what's up?'

'I can't explain now, but come as soon as you can and make it seem as if we'd arranged for you to come some time ago.'

'Ginny, you're being most mysterious,' began Katie.

'Must go, see you later,' interrupted Ginny, determined to give no explanations which might be overheard from the kitchen, and she rang off.

'That was my sister,' Ginny said brightly when she joined Harriet at the table. 'She's coming over later.'

'Will I see her?' asked Harriet between mouthfuls.

'It depends what time she gets here,' answered Ginny. 'You're going to bed early and then we'll decide what to do about you in the morning.'

★ ★ ★

Harriet was in the bath when Katie arrived, so Ginny was able to explain the situation to her sister in private.

'The thing is,' she finished, 'I don't want to leave her on her own while I go and find Gareth, especially if she realises where I'm going.'

'So you want me to baby-sit,' said Katie.

'Would you?' said Ginny gratefully.

'Of course,' said Katie, 'or I'll go and fetch him for you.'

'I thought of that,' said Ginny, 'but I must talk to him before he sees her and explain what's happened and why she ran away.'

'What about the grandmother?' suggested Katie. 'Wouldn't it be better to contact her? I mean, she might be more sympathetic.'

'I know, but there's no reply from her number. I've tried it several times. Harriet knows I've been ringing there. She doesn't seem to mind that, she was going to her grandmother anyway.'

When at last Harriet was tucked up in Ginny's bed, Ginny said to her, 'Now I have to go out for half-an-hour, but don't worry, Katie will stay here.'

'Where are you going?' asked Harriet apprehensively.

'Well, I can't get your grandmother on the phone because hers is out of order, so I thought I'd just pop across and tell her where you are so she doesn't worry. All right?'

Before Harriet could put up any objections Ginny continued, 'Katie'll be here with you if you need anything, but the best thing is to get a good night's sleep, and we'll sort all this out in the morning.'

★ ★ ★

Ginny hailed a cab and, giving the driver Gareth's address, sat back and prepared what she was going to say to him. She had hated having to lie to Harriet about her destination, but she knew Gareth must be told that the girl was safe as soon as possible, and Mrs. Chilton still didn't answer her phone. Ginny had even considered contacting the police to get them to tell him, but it would have blown everything up into a major drama.

All too soon, the cab drew up at Gareth's house and, getting out, Ginny asked the driver to wait. Though most of the house was in darkness there was a light on in a downstairs room and another in the outside porch. Ginny guessed Gareth was at home. She rang the bell and immediately the door was thrown open, as if Gareth had been waiting just inside it.

He looked pale and worried, but as he saw who was on the doorstep his expression cleared for an instant and he said, 'Ginny. It's you!'

'It's all right,' she said. 'I've got her. Harriet's safe in my flat.'

Gareth stared at her for a moment, uncomprehending, and then said, 'What do you mean, *you've* got her?'

'She came to me for help,' said Ginny simply. 'She's all right.'

'Thank God!' breathed Gareth leaning his head against the door for a moment. 'Thank God she's safe.'

'I've got a taxi waiting,' said Ginny.

'What?' Gareth glanced up again in surprise. 'Oh, don't worry. Come in a moment. I'll pay him off and we'll go in my car.'

Ginny stepped into the hall and

waited while Gareth dealt with the taxi, then he came in and closed the front door behind him.

'Come in here,' he said, leading the way into the lighted room. 'You say she's at your flat? Is she all right? She's not alone there, is she?'

'No, my sister Katie is with her and she's fine. She thinks I've gone round to see her grandmother.'

'Mother's away this weekend.'

'I know. Harriet went there first. It was when she found your mother wasn't there that she came on to me.'

'I see. But why didn't she come here?'

'Because she was afraid,' answered Ginny gently.

'Afraid!' cried Gareth. 'Afraid of me. Why, for heaven's sake?'

'She's not afraid of you, exactly,' explained Ginny, 'but she's terrified you'll send her back to that school.'

'Not that all over again. I've been over it with her so many times.' Gareth's relief at finding Harriet safe and well gave way to anger at the worry she had caused. 'She knows the situation,' he continued. 'She knows there isn't another solution at present.'

'I'll just ring the school and then I'll have to go round to Mother's.'

'But you said she was away,' said Ginny in surprise.

'She was,' said Gareth, 'with friends in the country, but I phoned her when the school phoned me. She's on her way back now in case Harriet turned up there.'

★　★　★

Ginny waited while Gareth telephoned the school, eavesdropping unashamedly. She wanted to know what he had in mind for Harriet's future. She learned little enough, but was relieved to hear him say he would come down with Harriet on Monday morning. At least the child would be able to spend the rest of the weekend with her grand-mother.

Ginny had already decided that Harriet should stay where she was for that night. It would be pointless to wake her now.

Ginny was prowling round the room as she listened and noticed, on the corner of the mantelpiece, the little carved squirrel. For a moment she stared at it and then picked it up, running a finger over its bushy wooden tail. She still liked it as much as when she had first bought it and had almost decided not to give it to Gareth. How long ago that all seemed.

★   ★   ★

She heard the telephone chink as Gareth put down the receiver, and she hastily replaced the squirrel and moved away from the mantelpiece. When Gareth came in she was studying a picture hanging in an alcove near the window.

'We'd better go,' he said. 'I'll fetch the car, it's in the lane at the back. You wait here in the dry and I'll bring it round.'

He disappeared into the damp night and Ginny waited in the hall for the car to come. As she waited, the telephone shrilled. For a moment she hesitated and then, thinking it might be Mrs. Chilton, she reached for the receiver, and said, 'Hello.'

A woman's voice said, 'Hello. Who's that? Is Gareth there?'

'No, I'm afraid he's not,' answered Ginny. 'He will be in a minute. He's just fetching the car.' The voice wasn't Mrs. Chilton's, Ginny was sure, but it sounded vaguely familiar. 'Who am I speaking to, please?'

'Angela Shaw,' replied the voice. 'Who are you?'

Of course it was Angela. Ginny was amazed she hadn't recognised that voice immediately.

'Virginia Howard,' she said coolly, though all her remembered dislikes boiled up inside her. 'Can I give him a message or will you hold on till he comes in?' she asked.

'Oh, it's you,' said Angela rudely. 'You just can't keep away from him, can you?'

Her laugh echoed down the line and Ginny simply replaced the receiver and cut off the sound. Then she went out of the door to wait for Gareth in the porch, and when the phone rang again she ignored it, merely closing the front door behind her.

Gareth pulled up outside at that moment, and she went down to the car.

As they drew out into the traffic, Ginny said casually, 'Angela Shaw rang. There was no message.'

'Angela did?' Gareth sounded surprised. 'What can she have wanted?'

'You, I imagine,' replied Ginny sweetly and then, changing the subject completely said, 'What about Harriet? You'll leave her to sleep the night where she is, I imagine.'

'I don't know. What do you think?'

'I think it would be best not to disturb him again tonight, and perhaps your mother could come for her in the morning. You'll be sending her back to school, I suppose?'

*   *   *

Ginny glanced sideways at Gareth and, by the head lamps of an approaching car, saw his lips tighten before he said, 'I know you don't approve, Ginny, and I don't like it myself, but I don't see what else I can do in the present circumstances.'

He looked so worried that, without thinking, Ginny put her hand on his arm and said, 'I'm sorry. I don't mean to criticise.'

She felt his arm stiffen under her hand and quickly drew away, clasping her hands in her lap to control a sudden tremor.

'Do you mind keeping her till the morning?' he asked.

'No, not at all. I really think it's the best plan. Especially if you let your mother take her home and meet her there quite casually.'

'Mmm, probably. I'll talk it over with Mother. One of us will come for her in the morning. Now, if you'll tell me exactly what Harriet told you, I shall be a little more in the picture when the time comes to make a decision.'

So Ginny related Harriet's tale and as she finished, realised with a jolt that they were pulling up outside her own house. Gareth got out at once and came round to open the passenger door. As she got out, he gave her his hand and then kept hold of hers for a moment.

'I won't come in, in case she's awake,' he said. 'Thank you for taking care of her, and for coming to find me. I'm very grateful.'

Ginny felt the colour flood her face and was glad the darkness concealed it. 'Don't be silly,' she said a little huskily. 'I'm glad to have been of help.'

'Even so, we're very grateful,' said Gareth and, bending his head, kissed her lightly on the forehead. He made no move to take her in his arms and search for her lips but, still holding on to her hand, walked with her to the front door.

'Mother'll be round for her first thing, I expect,' he said. 'Good night.'

'Good night, Gareth.'

Ginny let herself into the building and went upstairs to her own flat. Before opening the door, she took a deep breath, and then went in to face Katie.

When at last her sister had gone, Ginny looked in at the sleeping Harriet and then found her sleeping bag and spread it on the sofa. It was as she dozed off that the thought struck her. She hadn't told Gareth her address and yet he had driven straight here.

'I suppose he must have got it from the office files,' she thought. 'That's something else I'll have to see him about — another day.'

* * *

Mrs. Chilton arrived next morning in a taxi and was greeted enthusiastically by

212

Harriet. Ginny made coffee and the old lady stayed just long enough to drink it and to thank Ginny for all her kindness, before whisking Harriet away back to Knightsbridge.

'You'll be glad to hear David, at least, is well settled,' said Mrs. Chilton, 'and apparently has suffered no lasting ill effects from his escapade in Austria.' She laughed a little uneasily. 'You seem to make a habit of rescuing our children, Ginny.'

Ginny made a gesture of deprecation and Mrs. Chilton got awkwardly to her feet.

'Well, let me know how things go,' said Ginny and, kissing Harriet goodbye, saw them off in their taxi.

Ginny felt strangely discontented for the rest of the weekend. Time seemed heavy on her hands and she found her thoughts turning in a direction which disturbed her.

When she had overheard the awful conversation between Angela and Gareth in the hall of the *Haus Elisabeth*, Ginny had believed she felt such contempt for Gareth and his behaviour that nothing could ever dispel it or alter her attitude to him. Angela she had soon dismissed — she was not worth getting angry with. But in the few days she had spent with Gareth, Ginny had felt a bond grow between them, the first she had allowed to develop since Roger's departure from her life, and had been deeply humiliated at his casual exposure of it to Angela. Later, when Gareth had told her he loved her and talked of marriage, Ginny was still angry enough and hurt enough to turn him away in the bitterness of that humiliation, and if she had never seen him again, never heard him spoken of, she might never have regretted that dismissal and been free of him.

But she was not freed. Gareth continued to impinge upon her life, popping up in conversation, colliding with her in the street, providing her with a job, dealing with Harriet. It became more and more difficult not to think of him.

Ginny didn't want to analyse her feelings for him. She was afraid of what she might discover. Resolutely, she pushed him out of her mind, only to find he had infiltrated again when she had nothing particular to occupy her thoughts. She did wonder if Angela had rung yet again and managed to contact Gareth, and found herself hoping she had not. Up until now, Angela, as a person, had been irrelevant, but since the phone call she caused a feeling in Ginny which she would have recognised as jealousy had she paused to consider it. As it was, she dismissed it as residual dislike and tried to ignore it.

★ ★ ★

By the time Monday morning came, Ginny was very pleased the weekend was over. Work was what she needed — hard creative work to concentrate her mind to the exclusion of everything else. She reached the office early to begin the therapy, but she had finished up the work Nigel had given her on Friday and there was nothing for her to do. When Nigel himself came in he sent her out for an hour or so, saying she might as well get a coffee or something, but to be back by eleven for a meeting about a new client.

The meeting lasted until lunchtime, and then she began work, roughing out a few ideas. Quickly she became completely absorbed, and for a while was unaware of someone behind her watching as she drew with swift easy strokes. Then a shifting shadow made her glance up to find Gareth standing at her shoulder. Her heart thumped so hard as she discovered him there that she thought he must surely hear it.

'Hello,' she said huskily.

'I've taken her back,' he said without preamble.

Ginny laid down her pencil. 'Have you? How did she take it?'

'Not very well,' Gareth admitted, 'but I've promised that if she tries to make the best of it this term, I'll try and sort something out for next.'

'What kind of thing? I mean, what can you do?'

Gareth shrugged. 'I don't know yet. Mother and I are working on it. Neither of us realised quite how unhappy she was.'

'No. Well, perhaps you can find permanent living-in help so she can go somewhere locally as a day girl.'

'Maybe. We'll have to see.'

The conversation, had it been over-heard by a third party would have sounded stilted and awkward. Ginny found she didn't quite know what to say. She wanted to say something about his part in giving her this job, and yet somehow this wasn't the moment to mention it. Gareth looked tired and drawn and she realised that he didn't take his guardianship of his sister's children lightly. Perhaps he would ask her for a drink or something after the office closed and she could introduce the subject then. He didn't; for a moment he seemed about to say something else and then he changed his mind, merely adding more thanks for her help on Friday night.

He turned away and went into an inner office from which he did not emerge until everyone else, Ginny included, had gone home. She had waited a little after the office had begun to empty, but as there was no sign of him and she didn't want it to be apparent she was waiting, she left as well, her heart heavy with disappointment.

★　★　★

Gareth didn't come into the office again that week — at least not when Ginny was there — and, despite the fact that she was working on a job in conjunction with several others, she caught herself looking up every time the outer door opened, hoping to see him come in.

She came to the conclusion that Gareth was avoiding her, and it was not a conclusion that brought her any cheer. Obviously he was regretting his declaration in Austria as much as Ginny was regretting her haughty dismissal of it. Clearly he no longer felt anything but mild friendship for her. He had made no move to renew their earlier relationship, and he was not a man to pursue where he was once rejected.

At first Ginny had been relieved, but now she realised she minded his detachment, minded it more than she could have dreamed possible, minded it enough to be able to disregard the whispered conversation in the hall of the *Haus Elisabeth*, set it aside and forget it. And now it was too late. He had gone back to Angela.

When she got home on Friday evening, she found a letter waiting for her, addressed in a child's careful hand. A letter from Harriet. Ginny opened it, pleased that the little girl had written. The letter was short and to the point, but it drew from Ginny a smile of pleasure.

'Dear Ginny,

I am in the school concert next Saturday playing my reckorder. Uncle Gareth can't come becos he is going away. Please come. Here is a tiket. I have got a rabbit to look arfter now he is called Fluff.

Love from Harriet..
P.S. David is singing too.'

A small piece of pink card fell from the envelope with the date and time of the concert printed on it.

Thank goodness, thought Ginny as she re-read the letter; thank goodness Harriet had become involved in school activities at last. It really was a great pity Gareth couldn't go to the concert, it would have meant so much to Harriet to have him there. Still, she should certainly have one fan in the audience, and Ginny picked up a pen and replied at once to Harriet's letter, saying she would be delighted to come to the concert and was very much looking forward to meeting Fluff. She wondered whether to mention the letter to Gareth if she saw him, but decided not to. She didn't want to appear to be criticising him for not going himself.

★ ★ ★

In the event, the decision was of no consequence because the next evening Ginny was interrupted in what she was doing by a strident ringing on the doorbell. She had decided to paint the bathroom over the weekend, and was dressed in paint-smudged jeans and old sweat-shirt when she heard the bell. She glanced at herself in the bathroom mirror as she climbed down off the chair she was using as a ladder and saw she had paint on her nose and on the headscarf she had used to cover her hair.

She brushed an escaped wisp away from her forehead with the back of her hand, leaving another smear of paint across her forehead, and went to answer the doorbell's urgent summons. Whom she expected to see she was not quite sure, but it certainly was not Gareth. The moment she opened the door he strode into the flat, his face lined with worry, his dark eyes angry.

'Is she here?' he demanded, his eyes making a quick survey of the livingroom. 'Has Harriet come here?'

Ginny stared at him in surprise and then answered quietly, 'No, Gareth, she isn't. Has she run away again?'

'She's missing from school,' he replied briefly, then suddenly he dropped on to a chair, all the fight gone out of him. 'I was so sure she'd have come to you,' he said wearily. 'Where can she have gone this time?'

'Not at your mother's?'

'No, I've been there. There's no sign of her there or at my house. Where else would she go? Why would she go? She promised not to run away again — it was part of our bargain.'

'Perhaps she was disappointed because you couldn't go to see her concert.'

Gareth looked up in surprise. 'But I

am going,' he said. 'Of course I'm going. They're both in it.' He stared at Ginny for a moment and then asked, 'How did you know about it?'

Ginny handed him Harriet's letter and said, 'From this. Listen, you look as if you could do with a drink.'

Gareth glanced up from the letter. 'No, no, I haven't time. I must get back home in case she turns up there.' He half-rose from the chair but Ginny pushed him gently back into it.

'I'm going to make some coffee, and you're not leaving until you've drunk it. Or tea, if you prefer.'

Gareth seemed to accept her dictum. 'Coffee then. Thank you.'

★ ★ ★

Ginny was soon back with two steaming mugs of coffee and, sitting down in the chair opposite Gareth, she looked across at him, wishing she knew what to say or do to help. He sipped the coffee and, over the rim of the mug,

223

caught Ginny's eyes upon him. He gave a brief smile. For an instant his face was young and carefree, his eyes bright. For an instant he was the usual handsome attractive Gareth whom Ginny had come to love. She acknowledged it now as her heart contracted within her at his smile. She had known for days how she felt but, until this moment, had not brought herself to admit it. She returned his smile, sadly. It was too late.

'I seem to have interrupted you in the middle of something,' he said, indicating her painting clothes.

'I was just painting the bathroom,' said Ginny and, then afraid of silence, she went on, 'It hasn't been done for ages, I shouldn't think. I've certainly not redecorated in there. I did this room in the summer.' She glanced round the living-room.

'It's very nice,' said Gareth, hardly looking. 'I must go, Ginny, in case Harri turns up at home. Ring me if she comes here, won't you?' He got up.

'Of course,' replied Ginny. 'Leave me

your number, though. I haven't got it. That's why I had to come round last week.'

'Sure.' Gareth scribbled a number on the pad by the telephone.

'Let me know when you've found her.' Ginny said as she opened the front door. 'Oh, Gareth, what about her other grandparents. Would she go there?'

'The Croyds? But they live in Yorkshire. She'd never get there.'

'She might try. She stayed with them before, didn't she?'

'I suppose so. Well, I'll give them a ring when I get home. I don't want to raise the alarm too much. She's only been missing for four hours — she could well turn up here or at Mother's yet.'

Although his words were hopeful, Ginny could see he was extremely worried. After all, it didn't take four hours from the school to London — not in the train. She only hoped she hadn't tried to walk or accepted a lift.

'Had she any money?'

Gareth shrugged. 'I doubt it. Not a lot anyway. She spent all she had on last week's escapade. Mother probably gave her a little.'

He sighed and Ginny said softly, 'I know it's silly to say it, but try not to worry. I'm sure she'll be all right. I'll phone at once if she comes here.'

'Thanks, and I'll call you if I get any news.'

When he had gone down to his car, Ginny closed the front door and went back slowly into the sitting-room. She had lost all enthusiasm for her painting and idly she pulled the scarf from her head, shaking her hair free of its restraint. She sat in the chair Gareth had vacated, curling her feet up under her and stared unseeing into the empty room. Where on earth could Harriet be? Where would she go if not to her grandmother, Gareth or herself? Surely she wouldn't set out alone for Yorkshire.

Ginny wondered what new misery

had caused the little girl to run away again. 'If I were Harriet where would I run?' she asked herself. She didn't know the answer, and her helplessness weighed upon her mind. She was useless to all of them. Harriet hadn't turned to her this time and Gareth was beyond her reach. If she could have comforted him tonight, been able to give him strength and courage, she would have felt better. His face, strained and grey with worry, haunted her and she longed to soothe away the deep etched lines, but she knew it was too late.

★   ★   ★

How long she sat there unaware of her surroundings she didn't know. She lacked the incentive to turn and look at the clock, but she was still sitting there dry-eyed and cold, when the silence round her was shattered by the telephone. For a moment or two she let it ring, not wanting to speak to anybody and afraid it might be Katie. Katie was the last person she wanted to talk to, but the caller was insistent, not accepting that there was no reply, and at last she dragged herself to her feet and went to answer.

'Ginny?' Her heart missed a beat as she recognised the voice.

'Yes.'

'Sorry, have I got you out of bed or something?'

'No of course not. Any news?'

'Yes, thank heavens. They've found her. She's all right.'

Ginny could hear the happiness in his voice and cried, 'Oh, Gareth, that's marvellous. Where was she? Where had she gone?'

'She hadn't gone anywhere. She was locked in one of the outbuildings.'

'What!' Ginny was incredulous.

'Poor darling, she'd gone to see her new rabbit. We got it on Monday — several of the kids keep them and we thought it might give Harriet something to do. Anyway, apparently she went out

228

to say good night to him after tea, and while she was in the shed the gardener noticed the door was open, shot the bolt across and went on home. He's an oldish man and a bit deaf. He didn't hear her call, and she couldn't get out.'

'How awful,' said Ginny. 'She must have been terrified.'

'I think she was,' said Gareth, 'but it'd been late when she'd gone out there and she'd taken a torch, so she wasn't completely in darkness.'

'But how did they find her?'

'Luckily, one of the staff was coming in late and when Harriet heard the car she banged on the shed door with a garden trowel.'

'Thank goodness they found her,' said Ginny fervently. 'She might have been locked up out there all night.'

'Well, she's safely in bed in the san. now,' said Gareth. 'They're taking no chances, I promise you.'

'I'm sure,' said Ginny. 'Have you told her grandparents?'

'Yes, I've just rung them. They're all very relieved, of course, especially the Croyds. They were terrified she was struggling up to Yorkshire to find them.'

'Well, thank you for letting me know, Gareth. I'm very relieved, too.'

'Ginny?'

'Yes.'

'Look, I'm going down to see Harri tomorrow, just to make sure she's all right; you know, that this hasn't set us all back to square one.'

'I think that's a very good idea,' agreed Ginny.

'The thing is, well, will you come down with me? We could take them both out for the day. They'd love to see you, and I think you might well have a calming affect on Harriet if she's very upset by today's ordeal.'

He paused expectantly and Ginny felt her mind whirling, and it was with difficulty that she managed to speak calmly.

'Yes, of course, if you think I can help,' she said.

'Fine.' Gareth's voice, calm and controlled, gave nothing away. 'I'll pick you up at about eleven, if that's all right.'

'Fine,' echoed Ginny faintly.

6

Ginny spent some time choosing what to wear next day, trying on and discarding several outfits before settling for her favourite mulberry wool skirt topped with a matching polo necked jumper. A broad leather belt emphasised her neat waistline, and a pink scarf added a touch of colour at the neck. Ginny surveyed herself critically in the mirror when she had done her make-up. She was pleased with her appearance and, when she heard the ring of her bell at eleven o'clock precisely, she took a deep breath.

'Today's your last chance,' she told herself and, picking up her coat and bag, she opened the door.

Gareth helped her into her coat and, as he did so, he remarked, 'Hmm. You smell nice.'

Ginny laughed. 'Do I? Somebody

gave me this for Christmas.'

Gareth laughed, too. 'What good taste they must have,' he said, and led the way down to the car.

★ ★ ★

Once they were clear of London, Ginny watched the brown winter countryside slip past the window. It was a beautiful day, with pale yellow sun drenching the fields and promising warmer days to come. The first signs of spring were in the air and, though the trees and hedgerows were still stark and bare, occasional clumps of snowdrops stood bravely in wayside hollows, and patches of winter jasmine lent colour to the cottage gardens. The hopeful stirring of spring gave an added lift to Ginny's spirits, and she found herself smiling as she looked out of the window.

They spoke little on the journey, but the long silences that stretched between them weren't awkward or embarrassing, and both Ginny and Gareth were content to let them linger rather than force conversation.

When they drew in through the school gates and drove up to the front of the building, two children erupted from the main door and hurtled towards the car. Gareth pulled up and, leaping from the car himself, swept Harriet into his arms.

David, though a little more reserved, allowed himself an affectionate hug before drawing back and beaming up at his uncle.

'Look who I've brought with me,' said Gareth, setting Harriet down.

'It's Ginny, it's Ginny!' cried Harriet and, rushing round to the other side of the car, dragged the door open and pulled at Ginny to get out.

'I want to show Ginny my rabbit,' cried Harriet excitedly. 'Did you know I had a rabbit, Ginny?'

'Yes, I did.' Ginny smiled. 'You told me in your letter. I've written back to you. You should get it tomorrow or the next day.'

'Well, why don't I go and see the headmaster?' suggested Gareth. 'And you can be showing Ginny the rabbit.'

'Great,' shouted Harriet. 'Come on, Ginny, this way. Are you coming to the concert?' she asked as she skipped along beside Ginny.

'Yes, I've written to you about it. But, Harriet, Uncle Gareth says he's coming too. Why did you say he wasn't?'

Harriet stopped skipping and said, 'I wanted you to come, but I thought you wouldn't if Uncle Gareth was.'

'Why on earth not?'

'I don't know. Come on, Fluff's in here.'

Having duly admired Harriet's big black and white rabbit, Ginny said, 'Well, we'd better go back and find the men.'

★ ★ ★

Harriet paused a moment and then said, 'I got locked in here yesterday.'

'I know. I heard. What a brave girl

235

you must have been.'

'I banged and called but nobody came.'

'Nobody heard you, Harri,' said Ginny gently. She could see the little girl's eyes had filled with tears and she went on, 'I hope Fluff wasn't frightened.'

Harriet smiled at that. 'Oh, no,' she said, 'he kept me company. He thumped his feet when I banged with the trowel.'

'Look,' said Ginny, as they emerged from the shed, 'the others are waiting by the car.'

Harriet began to run. 'Race you!' she called over her shoulder, and dashed back to her uncle.

Ginny followed at half the speed and arrived a poor second, puffing and panting. Gareth laughed when he saw her and said, 'You *are* unfit.' He turned to the children. 'Well, come on,' he said. 'What are we waiting for?'

They had a marvellous day. Gareth found a pub with an excellent dining-room, and the children consumed an enormous lunch. They went for a long walk through some woods, squelching along the muddy paths, swinging on convenient branches, and playing hide and seek among the trees. Then they found somewhere for tea. Crumpets, toasted tea cakes and biscuits went the way of lunch, and at last even David admitted he couldn't eat any more.

'It's time we started back,' said Gareth carefully when everyone had finished. 'It's Monday morning tomorrow. Back to work!'

David groaned, but was obviously not really worried by the prospect.

Ginny waited for some reaction from Harriet, but all the little girl did was slip her hand into Gareth's and say, 'You will come and see me play my recorder, won't you?'

'I wouldn't miss it for the world,' he told her. 'Squeaks and all.'

The leave-taking at school was a little tearful, but it was only a week until Harriet would see them again and, with the promise that Ginny would come, too, she dried her eyes and went in with David.

★ ★ ★

Gareth drove them back to London, speaking little as he concentrated on the dark country lanes. Once safely on the main road, he said, 'I hope you don't mind about going to the concert. I'll drive you down, of course.'

Ginny smiled in the comforting darkness. 'No,' she said, 'I don't mind at all. I'd already written to Harriet to thank her for the ticket and to say I'd go.'

'I know,' said Gareth, 'but she sent you that under false pretences. Did you ever discover why, by the way?'

'No, not really.'

'No, nor did I.'

Ginny wondered if Gareth would suggest a meal or a drink on the way home. Not that she wanted either — she had had more than enough to eat with the children — but she was reluctant to let the day end and didn't relish a lonely evening in the flat. Gareth, however, suggested neither and drove her directly home, and when he pulled up outside the house she felt a sudden wave of desperation wash over her.

She couldn't let him just walk away now. She hadn't even thanked him for finding her a job. It was an excuse and she knew it, but she clutched it as a drowning man a straw.

Trying to keep her voice casual she said, 'Won't you come in for a minute, have a cup of coffee or something?' and when Gareth didn't reply at once, continued hastily, 'I'm sorry, I expect you've got a date this evening. Thank you for a lovely day. I think the children enjoyed it, don't you? Harriet seems more settled, now she's involved with things. Anyway — '

'Ginny, don't burble,' said Gareth with exasperation in his voice.

'What!'

'I'd love a coffee. Come on, it's cold out here.'

Together they climbed the stairs to the flat.

'Will you put the fire on while I make some coffee?' Ginny called brightly, having pushed Gareth towards the sitting-room and escaped into the kitchen.

He did so and switched on the television, too. When Ginny emerged from the kitchen with the coffee and a pile of sandwiches, he was dozing in the armchair, his feet stretched towards the fire, the television chattering unheeded in the corner.

While she had been hastily cutting the sandwiches, Ginny had come to a decision. Up until now she had decided to do nothing which might upset their precarious relationship until after Harriet's concert next week, but now she felt the opportunity to speak might not come again. In her heart she felt that any move must come from her after her stark rejection of Gareth in Austria. She was shaking as she considered the effrontery of what she was going to do, but, she reflected, one wasn't often given a second chance in such matters and she was determined to forget her pride and grasp the opportunity to speak up for herself.

Her heart was pounding as she entered the sitting-room with the tray. Gareth opened his eyes as she came in and said, 'Hope you don't mind me putting the television on. I thought we might catch the news.'

'No, that's all right.'

They sat and ate the sandwiches and drank their coffee while the news filled the screen. When it finished, Gareth got up and went to switch off the television.

'Nothing you wanted to watch was there?' he said, as he pressed the knob.

Ginny shook her head, her voice failed her — now was the time. Now or never. She cleared her throat and stood up, moving away to the window to tweak the curtains straight.

'Gareth,' she began, keeping her back to him. 'I — I wanted to thank you for finding me a job at the agency. I should have said something before, only, well I didn't know you'd helped at first and then — well, it was very kind of you.' She turned at last to face him and said, 'Particularly as we didn't part on the best of terms in Austria.'

★　★　★

Gareth was standing beside the fire, quite still, his face showing no emotion. Ginny felt almost sick with apprehension. If only he'd react. But he gave her no help at all.

'You said then — ' she faltered — 'you asked then if we could start again and I said . . . '

'You said no. I accepted that.' Gareth still didn't move.

Ginny almost lost her nerve at his quick interruption, but having got this far she had to go on. 'Now I want to ask the same of you, Gareth,' she said in a low voice. 'Please can we start again?'

'What would we be starting, Ginny?' he asked softly. The question hung between them for a moment and then he went on, 'An affair — no strings?'

Ginny swallowed hard. 'Like Angela? Oh, Gareth, no.'

The cry was ripped from her and in that instant Gareth was across the room and she was in his arms. She buried her face in his shoulder as her arms closed convulsively round him. Gently he lifted her chin and looked down at her, her face pale, her eyes luminous with unshed tears and her lips trembling.

'Oh, my Ginny, never like that. I love you too much,' he whispered and then he kissed her with all the longing and anguish of long denial, and Ginny, returning his kiss, found her head reeling at the demands of his lips.

★ ★ ★

At last they broke apart and, both shaking from the power of their emotion, they sank down together on the sofa, Gareth holding Ginny close to his heart and stroking her hair. She looked up at him, seeming about to speak, but then changed her mind.

'Tell me,' Gareth commanded pressing his lips to her face, 'what were you going to say?'

'Nothing.' Ginny shook her head. 'It doesn't matter now. I love you.'

'That'll do for a start.' He kissed her again and Ginny felt herself drowning in him, her happiness overwhelming her as she clung to him.

'Now tell me what went wrong,' he said gently. 'Before, I mean. I know it was my fault, but there was something more than just the arrival of Angela, wasn't there?' Ginny hesitated but Gareth said, 'Clean slate between us if we're starting again.'

So quietly, her arms about him, Ginny told Gareth about the conversation she'd overheard.

'Oh, my darling,' he groaned. 'I'm sorry. Why didn't you tell me before?'

'I couldn't,' replied Ginny in a low voice. 'I didn't want your scorn or, worse still, your pity.'

'Oh, my love. How I hurt you!' Gareth was filled with remorse. 'Can you really forgive me for being so stupid and cruel and thoughtless?'

Ginny took his hands in hers and held them to her cheeks. Then she looked up at him her eyes shining. 'I love you,' she said simply.

The truth shone between them for a full minute, then Gareth lowered his face to hers in a kiss of contrition, and Ginny knew that he was truly hers. alone.

'I'll tell you something,' said Gareth a little later. 'Nigel's going to be pleased we've sorted ourselves out.'

'Nigel?' said Ginny in surprise.

'Yes, he said the other day he hadn't had a sensible word out of either of us for days. You were as jumpy as a kitten, concentration all to pot, and I couldn't string two consecutive thoughts together. I couldn't get you out of my mind. I knew I'd have to speak to you again soon. Last night when you sat over there, I could hardly keep my hands off you, but I was so afraid of scaring you off.'

'I thought you'd changed your mind,' said Ginny in a small voice. 'I thought you regretted what you'd said in Austria.'

'Never.' A simple word but to Ginny eminently satisfactory.

'What will your Angela say?'

'I haven't got an Angela,' replied Gareth in an injured tone, his eyes brimming with laughter. 'She hasn't spoken to me, actually, since she swept out in Austria.'

'She tried to the other day,' Ginny reminded him. 'I took the call.'

'So she did! Well, perhaps she'd already tired of the next lucky fellow and was trying to make a comeback.'

'Perhaps — ' began Ginny.

'Perhaps,' said Gareth firmly, 'we should forget all about her and talk of more important things.'

'Us?' she said, snuggling more closely against him.

'Yes, us,' he said, squeezing her tightly. 'To begin with, there's the children. We'll tell them when we go to the concert on Saturday,' said Gareth when he had finished kissing her again.

'Tell them what?'

'That we're getting married.' His eyes held hers for an instant. 'We are, aren't we?'

'If you want me,' answered Ginny, her voice shaky as she saw the need in his eyes.

'I want you,' said Gareth huskily, 'more than anything else in the world. Remember that always. Promise?'

And Ginny promised.

THE END

We do hope that you have enjoyed reading this large print book.

Did you know that all of our titles are available for purchase?

We publish a wide range of high quality large print books including:
Romances, Mysteries, Classics
General Fiction
Non Fiction and Westerns

Special interest titles available in large print are:
The Little Oxford Dictionary
Music Book, Song Book
Hymn Book, Service Book

Also available from us courtesy of Oxford University Press:
Young Readers' Dictionary
(large print edition)
Young Readers' Thesaurus
(large print edition)

For further information or a free brochure, please contact us at:
Ulverscroft Large Print Books Ltd.,
The Green, Bradgate Road, Anstey,
Leicester, LE7 7FU, England.
Tel: (00 44) **0116 236 4325**
Fax: (00 44) **0116 234 0205**

Other titles in the
Linford Romance Library:

AT SEAGULL BAY

Catriona McCuaig

When Florence Williams and her
sister Edie inherit houses at Seagull
Bay they decide to set themselves up
as seaside landladies, catering to
summer visitors. There, Florence's
daughters become mixed up with
two wildly unsuitable young men.
Flattered by the attentions of an
unscrupulous entertainer, Vicky tries
to elope, but is brought back in
time. Having learned that holiday
romances seldom last, her prim
sister, Alice, wonders if true love will
ever come her way.

A TIME TO RUN

Janet Whitehead

When nurse Lynn Crane finds employment at an isolated manor house in the Yorkshire countryside, all is not what it seems. As she nurses her attractive patient, Serge Varda, Prince of Estavia, an alarming truth emerges: her employers, Max Ozerov and the sinister Dr Miros, his countrymen, plan to wrest control of the country from him. The young couple escape from almost certain death, but, as Serge is eventually restored to state duties, will he share them with Lynne?